Dear Readers,

I still remember the first tin the godfather of street lit. He was the first to write books about characters I could identify with. To some, the stories may have been aggressive, overly stylized, and even dangerous. But there was an honesty there—a realness. I made a vow that if I wrote a book or got into the publishing game, I would try the same one-two punch—that of a Daddy Cool or Black Gangster.

Last year, my memoir, *From Pieces to Weight*, marked the beginning. Now I'm rounding up some of the top writers, same way I rounded up some of the top rappers in the game, to form **G-Unit** and take this series to the top of the literary world. The stories in the **G-Unit** series are the kinds of dramas me and my crew have been dealing with our whole lives: death, deceit, double-crosses, ultimate loyalty, and total betrayal. It's about our life on the streets, and no one knows it better than us. Not to mention, when it comes to delivering authentic gritty urban stories of the high and low life, our audience expects the best.

That's what we're going to deliver, starting with **Nikki Turner**, bestselling author of *A Hustler's Wife* and *The Glamorous Life*; **Noire**, bestselling author of *G-Spot* and *Thug-A-Licious*; and finally **K. Elliott**, author of *Street Fame*.

You know, I don't do anything halfway, and we're going to take this street lit thing to a whole other level. Are you ready?

G Unit
Books

THE SKI MASK WAY

50 Cent
and K. Elliott

POCKET BOOKS, a division of Simon & Schuster, Inc.
1230 Avenue of the Americas, New York, NY 10020

This book is a work of fiction. Names, characters, places and incidents are products of the author's imagination or are used fictitiously. Any resemblance to actual events or locales or persons, living or dead, is entirely coincidental.

ISBN-13: 978-1-4165-3101-2
ISBN-10: 1-4165-3101-7

First G-Unit/Pocket Books paperback edition January 2007

10 9 8 7 6 5

POCKET and colophon are registered trademarks of Simon & Schuster Inc.

Manufactured in the United States of America

For information regarding special discounts for bulk purchases, please contact Simon & Schuster Special Sales at 1–800–456–6798 or business@simonmandschuster.com.

To my uncle Ronnie Douglas,
may he RIP.

Acknowledgments

First I would like to thank God for continuing to open doors as I continue to pursue my dreams. My mother and father, Otis and Margaret Douglas, thanks for the support and encouragement. Aisha Lindsey, thanks for being there for me. I would like to thank Marc Gerald for presenting me with this wonderful opportunity. MTV, G-Unit, and Simon and Schuster, thanks for the opportunity to present my work to the masses. 50 Cent, thanks for your vision. Lauren McKenna, you were wonderful to work with, and I hope we get a chance to do this again someday.

The following authors I would like to acknowledge: Hallema Simmons, Shawna A Grundy, S. W. Smith, Kwan, Nikki Turner, Thomas Long, Jihad, LaJill Hunt, Danielle Santiago, Tushonda Whitiker, T. N. Baker, Shannon Holmes, Erik Gray, Mark Anthony, Brandon McCalla, Treasure Blue, and anybody else that I may have forgotten that I have met along the way.

Thanks to the following bookstores: Dynasty Books,

Hue-Man Books, Karibu, and the Walden Book chain, thanks to your continued support of K Elliott.

I would also like to acknowledge Power 98 radio station of Charlotte, North Carolina, thank you for your support. Artie, the one-woman party, thank you for all the love and support. To Nakia Murray of Literary Consulting Group, we're on the next level, baby, your boy is about to shine. Last but not least, my man Channing Ford, much love to you. Though we have our ups and downs on the road, we handle our business; nobody in the game can sell out a store like our team.

This one is dedicated to all those who are positive.

CHAPTER 1

The fruit punch–red Impala had gold Dayton rims. The car gleamed so much, you could see your reflection in the hood. The interior was cream-colored leather. The car had been totally restored. The Impala was the only one that Butter owned and he cherished it. He and Seven sat on the hood of his car, smoking purple haze, listening to Mobb Deep's "Shook Ones Part I."

"This was my shit back in the day and those niggas was from round my way," Seven said.

Butter puffed the blunt. "You knew them?"

Seven reached for the blunt. "Well, not exactly. My manz in'nem used to hang with Prodigy; but, naw, I ain't know them, but I seen them a few times."

"I listen to them, when I'm about to do a lick, you know?" Butter pulled out a .380 and cocked the hammer. "It gets my adrenaline going, you know?"

"Man, put that gun away," Seven said.

"What, nigga? You scared of guns? How the fuck is you from New York and you afraid of guns?"

"Naw; I ain't afraid of guns—just high, careless niggas with guns."

Butter put the gun on safety.

"I didn't know niggas in the South was into that Mobb Deep shit."

Butter looked confused. He didn't say anything, he just puffed. Finally he couldn't control his thoughts or his tongue.

"You know what? Y'all New York niggas always think that we slow down here. I can relate to Mobb Deep."

"I feel ya," Seven said. "Calm down, son. I mean, I ain't mean it like that." Seven did think southern niggas were slow, once upon a time, before he'd gone to Virginia. He'd met some real gangsters in Virginia. Butter seemed to be thorough. He'd met him at a temp agency where they both were applying for a job and started talking. After a fifteen-minute conversation he realized they had a lot in common: They both were street niggas and ex-cons.

"So what you're all-time favorite gangster movie?"

"*Dead Presidents*."

"I expected you to say *King of New York*, *New Jack City*, *Menace II Society*. Never did I expect you to say this."

Butter inhaled the haze and then coughed. "Yeah, I liked that movie."

"I liked *Paid in Full*, myself," Seven said.

Butter coughed again "Yeah, that shit was crazy; those mufukas was making a lot of money."

"You know what my favorite scene was?"

"What?"

"You know the scene where Mitch calls Rico and tells him he has coke and Rico flips and kills his man for the work?"

"Why is that your favorite scene?" Butter asked.

"Because the lesson learned is niggas will kill you for life-changing money. My daddy always told me two things: Your friends will kill you for the right price, and every bad guy likes to think of himself as good," Seven said

"Was you and your pops smoking weed when he told you that shit? Sounds like that weed philosophy," Butter commented.

"That's real talk, man, from a man who's doing life in the pen."

"That's why you gotta watch everybody." Butter blew out a huge smoke ring, pulled the gun out, cocked it again, then kissed the barrel. "I'm 'bout hit a lick tonight, man. I needs some money in a major way."

"I ain't got shit myself, and that motherfuckin' baby

mama is nagging the shit out of me. My son is two and can't walk—he needs physical therapy. The bitch ain't got no insurance." Seven thought about his boy and other problems he was having. He hardly ever had money. Sometimes he would detail cars for hustlers, but he didn't have any real paper—not like he was used to—hell, before he'd gotten locked up he had thousands of dollars on him at all times. Now it was down to this petty-assed car-washing—he felt like a sucker.

Butter sat back on the Impala. Young Jeezy was now coming from the Chevy. "You know what? I thought you were locked up three years ago in Virginia. Right."

"Yeah."

"How the fuck did you get her pregnant, anyway? I mean, I was thinking about that shit one night. I was high as fuck, sitting outside, looking up at the sky and shit. You know that's when you high; you have the strangest thoughts."

"Now that's got to be a weed-induced thought."

"I was on that purple haze and my mind was just racing and shit, and I was thinking of all kinds of stupid shit."

"Well, Adrian was actually a guard that I met while I was on the inside. I started banging her and the warden got wind of it. Fired her and put me in solitary confinement," Seven said.

Butter's eyes grew wide. "Nigga, quit lying."

"I'm serious. One thing about me, man, is that I've never

had a problem with the ladies, I've always been able to pull them." Seven was indeed a ladies' man. Very attractive dark smooth skin, wavy hair; his body was well-defined and his teeth were eggshell white. The women loved him.

"Damn, that's an amazing story." Butter said.

"Yeah, man. That's how the shit went down. I got her pregnant. We kept in touch while I was in prison and she moved to Charlotte, N.C., so that's why I relocated here."

"Why did you relocate here?"

Seven inhaled the blunt. "Damn, nigga, you a news reporter? Motherfucker, why so many questions—you the FBI or something?"

"Naw, just making sure *you* ain't FBI," Butter replied.

"I mean I got three sisters and three brothers in New York, but I ain't really fucking with them like that. I mean, the whole time I was down only one of my sisters came to visit me so I ain't really have no reason to go back to New York, and I ain't going back to Virginia cuz all my niggas locked up."

"Damn. You came all the way down here not knowing anybody."

"I wasn't afraid. The only thing I was worried about was that bitch tripping, and she tripped and put me out. But, it's okay, I got my own room in the boardinghouse and I got some pussy, so I'm good."

"Nigga, you must not be used to having money."

"Now that's where you're wrong at. I made a lot of money. Ran with a fucking crew—and most of them niggas that I ran with are either dead or in jail."

Butter rolled another blunt, lit it and inhaled, then blew another smoke ring before coughing loudly. "What the fuck were y'all doing?"

"Coke, heroin, e-pills . . . all types shit."

"I can't believe that shit, man, cuz it just seems like you are so content with being a average motherfucker."

"Nigga, *you* average," Seven said.

"But I ain't never got no real money, nigga. I bet y'all seen millions."

Seven thought back. A few years ago he was driving Porsches, BMWs and shit with expensive rims. Ever since he'd been released from prison a year ago, it had only been a bus pass. He really wanted money, too, but he didn't know anybody who would give him drugs. He was in Charlotte. Nobody knew him. This was both good and bad. It was good because he didn't have a reputation to keep, but it was bad because he couldn't get anybody in Charlotte to supply him.

Butter passed Seven the gun. "Got this motherfucker for two rocks, nigga, it was brand-new in the box."

"What you mean you got it for two rocks, you ain't no hustler."

"I know but I have drugs because I'm the type of motherfucker that takes shit from the dope boyz, you know, if they making money I'm making money because they have to give me money or else I'll rob they punk ass. I actually took the dope from a nigga, gave it to another motherfucker for the gun and when I got the gun I robbed the nigga that sold me the gun and got my rocks back . . . that's how ya boy Butter gets down."

Seven laughed but he really didn't think that was funny. He'd been around niggas like Butter before and knew he could only trust him as far as he could see him.

"So—do you want to help me with this lick?"

"So, who is this cat, Caesar? And does he have money?"

"He has a Colombian plug, and word in the street is he gets those bricks for thirteen five. He just bought this stripper bitch a Benz for her birthday."

"How can we get at him?" Seven wanted to know. He remembered the days when he was dealing in Richmond, Virginia. He knew that the streets talk, especially in the south; news spread like wildfire. Things that were just ordinary conversation could be made into major news. He also knew that whoever Caesar was, it wasn't going to be easy to get to him.

"One thing you have to always remember is that most of these major drug dealers are cowards. You don't have to worry about them. It's the niggas around them that you have to worry about; the enforcer-type niggas. Those are the hungry mufuckas that will do something to you," Butter pointed out.

"Exactly. I know this. I mean I ain't never stuck nobody up, but I know the fuckin' streets. I know legendary stickup kids in New York. I'm talking about kidnap-your-mom type niggas, son."

Butter chuckled to himself. He never understood why New Yorkers called everybody "son." A motherfucker could be seventy years old and still be called son.

"I know what ya mean. But—back to the business. You with me or not?"

Seven thought for a moment and took a puff of the blunt. He knew that if what Butter said was true, he would be doing a lot better than he had been doing. Hell. He lived in a boardinghouse with twelve other sweaty men and one crackhead woman. He wanted out of that place more than he did prison. He envisioned taking kilos of coke from the drug dealer with the Colombian connection. "Yeah. I'm down, son."

Butter tossed him a pair of gloves and a ski mask and a sawed-off pump shotgun. "Let's get that money the fast way—the ski mask way."

"The ski mask way . . . Hell yeah." Seven said. He and Butter high-fived.

■

The subdivision was called Peaceful Oaks. A quiet neighborhood in the southeastern part of Charlotte. It was predominantely white, which meant they had to be very cautious. White people called the police at the slightest bit of suspicion. Two black men rolling through suburbia after midnight was not a good look. Butter and Seven rolled through the neighborhood looking out for Good Samaritans—people that wanted to be on the news saying that they tipped the police.

Caesar's street was Peaceful Way Drive. Butter went one street over, to Peaceful Pine Drive, and parked the car in the driveway of an abandoned house. He and Seven hopped over the privacy fence in the backyard into Caesar's backyard and looked around, but didn't see anybody. Then Seven saw the sign that read ADP in front of the door.

"He has an alarm. Man. What do we do about that?"

"He has a baby, too."

Seven looked confused. "What the fuck does that have to do with anything?"

"Don't worry about this shit. I've done it before. I got this player."

Seven put on the mask and the gloves. He thought about

prison: the sick old men there, the perverts, the liars and the snitches. He didn't want to go back to that place. They went around front. Nobody noticed them and the street was dark.

"On the count of three, I'm going to kick in the door. I want you to go in one room and I go in the other, just in case there *is* somebody else in the house."

"Nigga, you've done this shit before for real?" Seven said.

Butter's face hardened. "This ain't no fuckin' game to me, man. I need to eat."

"Okay. Let's do it."

Butter kicked the door in and ran into the first bedroom.

Seven ran into the second bedroom and found a man and a woman on the floor, naked. He pointed the gun at the man. "Okay, I need you to get the fuck up and your bitch to stay on the floor with her hands on her head."

The man was shaking and it looked as if tears were in his eyes. *Damn, what a bitch-assed nigga,* Seven thought.

"Nobody is going to get hurt as long as long as you do what the fuck I say."

Butter walked into the room with a little boy wearing Elmo pajamas.

"Look what I have."

The little boy began to cry.

The alarm went off. Caesar said, "The police will be here soon. You don't want to go to jail, do you?"

Seven said sarcastically, "Yeah. That what we came here for . . . to get caught and go to jail." He slapped Caesar with the barrel of the gun.

"Don't you say a motherfuckin' thing."

He walked Caesar into the hallway to the alarm keypad.

"Disarm the alarm," Seven ordered.

Caesar punched in the code.

The telephone rang. Butter picked it up without answering it. The caller ID said ADP.

"The fuckin' alarm company."

"Well, we knew they had an alarm," Seven said.

"Don't worry," Butter said, and he walked the phone over to Caesar with the infant still in his hand, crying. "Tell them everything is okay," Butter said, "If you try some slick shit, I'll blow your fucking block off, nigga."

"Hello," Caesar said.

A female voice said, "This is ADP. Is everything okay?"

"Yes, everything is fine. I just didn't get to the alarm pad on time."

"Okay. What is your password?"

"My password?"

Butter clenched his teeth.

"Tell the bitch your password or else it's going to be a fuckin' bloodbath in this motherfucker. I promise you, man."

"The password is 'rubber.'"

The little boy started crying louder.

"Okay, sir. Are you sure everything is okay?"

"Yes; everything is fine, ma'am."

"Do I hear a child crying?"

"That's my son. The alarm scared him."

"Okay, sir. You have a good night."

Butter snatched the phone out of Caesar's hand and terminated the call.

"Okay, man. Where the fuck is the dope, nigga?"

"Ain't no dope here, man."

"Okay, motherfucker. You think I'm stupid?" Seven said through clenched teeth. "You think I believe you *worked* for this house and that fat-assed Benz you got outside? You think that I think this fine-assed bitch is with you for you good looks?" Seven looked at the female, who was still face-down and shaking nervously.

"Where the fuck is the cash?" Butter said.

"I'm telling you I ain't got shit."

"Nigga, you ain't gonna have no fuckin' son if you don't give us what we want."

"Please don't hurt my baby," the woman said, then stood.

Seven pointed the gun at her.

"Bitch, get back on the floor."

"Where the fuck is the dope?" Butter repeated.

"There ain't no dope here."

Butter walked over to the window and pulled the curtains back. "I'ma count to three. If you don't give me some dope or some money, this little boy is going out of the window."

"Put the child down," Seven said as he thought about his own little boy. He never had a soft spot for kids until he had brought Tracey into the world.

He and Butter made eye contact before Butter said, "Nigga, you don' tell me what the fuck to do. I'm telling this motherfucker if I don't get what the fuck I want, this little boy is going out of the window."

The woman stood and Seven aimed the gun at her again. "Get your ass back on the floor."

"No. Please, please don't hurt my baby. I'll tell you where the money is."

Seven cocked the hammer of the gun. "Well, tell me where the goddamned money is, then."

"Please, put my son down first."

Butter put the child on the bed.

The woman went into the closet and pulled out a large green gym bag. Butter unzipped the bag and saw bundles of money. He zipped the bag back up.

"Okay; where's the dope, bitch?"

"There really ain't no dope in here. I swear to God," the woman said.

"Okay."

Butter stepped out of the closet.

"Bring him to me," Butter said to Seven.

Seven walked Caesar over.

"Okay, nigga. Where ya fucking car keys at, and ya guns and shit?"

The woman got the keys from the nightstand and handed them to Butter.

Butter duct-taped Caesar's hands and feet together and handcuffed the woman to the bed.

The baby was still crying. Seven walked over to him, ran his fingers through the toddler's hair and said, "It's going to be okay."

They left with the money.

CHAPTER 2

Elise worked at the Adam's Mark Hotel. She'd been there for two months and she had hated every minute of it, but she had promised her mom that she would stop stripping and get a real job. She couldn't believe that two weeks of hard work amounted to only about $640. She had made that and more in one night at the Peaches and Cream Cabaret. This weekend was particularly annoying. The CIAA tournament was in town. Celebrities from all over were there to party and enjoy themselves. Along with the celebrities were the ballers, and here she was—stuck at the damn hotel working when she should have been out partying or, at the very least, hanging with Seven, her New York boyfriend. After all, he had some money this weekend. He'd given her a thousand dollars to help her pay bills. She wondered where the money had come from, because one minute the nigga was broke, and the next minute he had a new car and money at his disposal. When she asked, he simply said, "A lick." That was what she liked about men like Seven—they lived on the edge and weren't afraid to hustle or take. But ever since she'd known Seven he'd struggled financially. He told her he'd just gotten out of prison in Virginia for drug charges, but Elise wasn't stupid: She'd seen men like Seven get out of prison, find a connection and get rich. She was a smart girl, she knew it would just be a matter of time before Seven started making money again. She wanted to be down for him while he was still struggling, though she hated going to that damn boardinghouse where he lived with all those roaches and crackheads; but she was hanging in there for Seven. Besides, he was cute and he treated her well when he had money, which was not often.

She figured it must have been some kind of heist, because her girlfriend Candy used to fuck Seven's friend Butter, and he was known as a stick-up kid. She decided that she wasn't going to press the issue.

■

His platinum American Express card said Reggie Walker; his license said he was from St. Louis, Missouri. He was wearing a velour Sean John sweat suit; on his wrist was a presidential Rolex with a diamond bezel. Elise noticed this right away. She thought, *This watch must have cost at least fifty thousand dollars.*

"Hello, beautiful," he said.

Elise smiled, and took his credit card and gave him a check-in form.

"You know what? I want to take you out. How can I get a date from yo' sexy ass?"

She blushed again, then said, "I don't know if your game is tight. Maybe we can get together. How long you in town for?"

"Three, maybe four days," Reggie said, and then he picked up his Louis Vuitton briefcase from the floor—an obvious attempt to impress Elise.

"I don't know. We'll see."

Reggie smiled. "I mean, it's no big deal. I thought you were kind of fly for a country girl."

"What the fuck do you mean, country? St. Louis is country-ass hell."

"Lets face it, ma. You from a small city. It's no big deal." Reggie smiled. "I just wanted to introduce you to the finer things in life, but you ain't ready for this," he said as he picked up his suitcase and headed to his room.

Elise looked around. She wanted to curse him out badly, but Rob the manager was standing behind her. She was already on probation with the company for having been late too many times and hooking her friends up with rooms. She just held her breath. But nothing happened.

On her break, she called Seven. "Yeah, this nigga in here from St. Louis. The motherfucker has some serious money, baby."

"Oh yeah? How do you know?"

"Cuz; he had Louis Vuitton luggage, a Rolex, platinum cards, and the fool had the nerve to pull out a wad of money saying he wanted to take me shopping."

Seven smiled to himself. He wondered why niggas were so stupid, always trying to impress women with their money. This was most niggas with money's worst mistake. "You think he can be touched, huh?"

"For sho'; and I'm gonna help you touch. I'll make you a copy of his room key."

"Don't talk on phones like that."

"Oh, baby. I'm sorry."

"Just call us when he leaves for the night to go party."

"Okay."

■

It was 10:30 P.M. when Mr. St. Louis strolled the lobby dressed impeccably in a pinstripe Calvin Klein blazer, jeans, and yet another expensive watch—this time it was a Cartier dripping with diamonds. He winked at Elise and walked out the front door of the hotel. Elise followed to see what he was driving—a rented Porsche Cayenne truck. *Yes, this nigga is a baller*, she said to herself

She called Seven immediately. He picked up on the second ring.

"Hello."

"Mr. St. Louis is out for the evening."

"Oh yeah? Me and Butter will be right over."

"Okay. Cool."

Seven and Butter arrived thirty minutes later, and Elise gave Seven the key to Reggie's room.

It was four in the morning when Mr. St. Louis returned to the hotel, back from a long night of drinks and parties and a little purple kush. He was tired and high. He couldn't wait to get to his bed. He stood in front of his door for five minutes trying to put his car key in the room door.

■

Butter and Seven were waiting in the bathroom with ski masks and black gloves on. They were starting to get very impatient.

"What the fuck is going on out there?" Seven asked.

"The nigga probably drunk," Butter said.

Finally, St. Louis realized that he needed to use a card and not a key to get into the room. When he opened the door Butter greeted him with a sawed-off shotgun.

"Strip, nigga, or you will be in hell in the next five seconds."

St. Louis threw his hands up in the air. "What the fuck is going on?" He turned and attempted to walk out of the door but Butter slapped him with the butt of the gun. Blood shot from his head. St. Louis peed on himself he was so nervous.

"Lay the fuck down or it's gonna be all over for you, nigga," Butter said.

Seven came out the bathroom with duct tape in his hand.

"Let me see your hands."

St. Louis held out his hands. Seven duct-taped the man's hands together, sat him on the bed and pulled his pants off.

"Where the fuck is the money, nigga?"

"It's in my pocket. I have five thousand dollars in my pocket," St. Louis blurted.

"Five thousand dollars? That ain't gonna buy shit, nigga. You better come up with something else or I'ma hurt you, man."

Butter's eyes were red through the mask. He was wearing his grill that was laced with canary diamonds. And he very much looked like the lunatic that he really was.

"I don't have no cash, man. I swear to you, this is all I brought."

"Stand up," Butter ordered while at the same time forcing him to his feet.

The man stood. His hands were still taped. Butter walked him out to the balcony. They looked out over the city. The room was on the forty-second floor. "I will push your ass off this balcony if you don't come up with something for me."

"I have a watch, man, and a ring that's valued at about seventy-five thousand. That's all I got."

"Let me see that watch, man," Seven said.

St. Louis held out his wrist and Seven slipped the watch over his hand.

Butter looked at the watch then asked, "What do you think the watch is worth?"

"At least fifty thousand," Seven said.

"Okay. What else do you have, nigga?"

"Nothing," St. Louis answered.

"No rings or other jewelry?"

"No."

"Now how you going to have a piece like this with no rings or shit."

St. Louis shrugged. "I'm just a really plain dude, man. I don't like jewels and shit, for moments like these."

"Okay. I believe you."

Butter checked this nigga's briefcase.

"Where's the key to the briefcase?" he asked.

"There ain't nothing in the briefcase."

Butter pointed the shotgun back at him. This time the barrel was right below his nose.

"I didn't ask you that. I want to know where the fuck the key is."

"My pants pocket. It's the little gold one."

The opened briefcase revealed a wad of hundred-dollar bills.

"Look at what I have here."

"Okay. This is all of it," St. Louis said.

Butter slapped him in the mouth with the gun, and Seven kicked him in the ribs.

"Oh, my God. Please don't hurt me."

"You see? It didn't have to be like this, man. All you had to do was tell us where the money was. Instead you want to be hard, and this is what you get."

Butter unbuttoned St. Louis's shirt, snatched a small chain with a diamond cross from his neck, then pulled his socks off. Grabbing him by the arm, he told Seven to hold the other arm. They walked him to the balcony, duct-taped his feet together and left him there in nothing but his underwear.

■

Seven and Butter counted the money at Butter's apartment. The total was $9,876, including the nearly $5,000 he had in his briefcase. They split the money evenly. But then Seven suggested that they give Elise a thousand for putting them up on the heist. Butter looked annoyed.

"Give her money? That's *your* bitch. Why don't *you* give her money?"

Seven didn't respond immediately.

"So you don't want to give her nothing?" he said finally.

"For what?" Butter said as he counted his money again.

"For helping us out. Don't you see? If we pay her, she'll do it again, or at least help us out."

Butter peeled off five hundred-dollar bills and said, "I ain't giving her none of the money from the jewelry."

"She don't have to know about the jewelry. But I think she's smart. She actually told me he had a Rolex on."

"Oh yeah?"

"Yes."

"Okay. This bitch can be good for the team. I see what ya mean."

They gave each other five.

"We gonna do it big out here, nigga," Butter said. "I have another target. He has money, but he has a little security staff. It's not going to be easy to get to him."

"What's the nigga's name?" Seven asked.

"Reno. Yeah, he's a big fat motherfucker."

"He connected like Caesar?"

"I think it's not so much his connect but his hustle. I mean, he has workers all over town. The man has crazy hustle, you know what I mean?"

"Can we use Elise to get next to him?"

"I don't know, but it's worth a try. He's in Club Champagne on Wednesday night for topless boxing."

■

Later that evening Seven visited his child. Seven's son's name was Tracey. Adrian, his baby's mother, was into unisex names. Seven wasn't—not for boys, anyway—but there was nothing he could do about that. He wasn't with Adrian when she delivered the baby. He was finishing his prison sentence. Adrian and Tracey lived in the Ivy Apartments, in a nice one-bedroom apartment.

Seven rang the door bell. Two minutes later Adrian opened the door with a white terry-cloth robe on and rollers in her hair. She was a pretty woman, very petite in stature, and she rarely wore makeup.

"So, what do you want?"

"I came to see my son."

She stepped to the side and invited him in. The apartment was very tiny but it was tidy. Seven sat on the couch next to the small TV. "So where is my boy?"

"He's asleep. I'll go get him."

About three minutes later, Adrian reappeared carrying the little boy. Adrian woke Tracey. He smiled when he saw his father and held his hands out. He wanted to be held by his dad. Seven grabbed the boy.

"How's my little man?"

"Daddy," Tracey said as a huge smile appeared on his face.

Seven attempted to stand Tracey up on the floor but the child's legs were bowed severely. He had Blount's disease, which hindered his ability to walk. Little Tracey struggled to take a step but he fell and started crying. Seven picked him up and tossed him up into the air three times before he started grinning.

"That's Daddy's big boy," Seven said. He laid little Tracey on the sofa and then looked at Adrian.

"I just want my boy to walk."

Her face became solemn.

"I know, but he's going to need to get braces on his legs, and I just don't have the money or insurance for them."

"How much are the braces going to cost?"

"I signed up for Medicaid. They are going to pay for them, you know, but it's the surgery and the physical therapy that's going to be the problem."

"I got some money but I don't know if it's enough," Seven responded, thinking about the two heists he and Butter had pulled off. He thought about the other drug dealer that Butter had talked about, wondered how much money he would have. He didn't really like this little robbing career that he'd embarked upon, but he knew he had to get his son help.

"After the braces come off he will still need an operation, if we ever want him to be almost normal," Adrian said.

Seven took a deep breath. He didn't say anything, but he knew he had to come up with money, and fast. His little boy was growing quickly. Before long he'd be three and he would still be behind the other kids.

"All that is good, but right now I need help with the day care. Do you have money for that?" Adrian said angrily.

"Haven't I always helped you?"

"Do you really want me to answer that question?" Her hands were now on her hips.

Seven didn't say anything—he just pulled out a wad of money and peeled off eight hundred-dollar bills. Her eyes grew big.

"Where did you get all that money from?"

"Don't worry about it."

Adrian took the bills and folded them. Then she said, "Seven, you damn sure better not be selling no drugs again."

"Ain't nobody selling no drugs."

She huffed. "Okay. This will only make the situation

worse. You know what I mean?" Adrian put the money in her bra, then sat beside Tracey on the sofa. "Well, I'm not going to ask you what you did to get the money; I don't care, but I don't want my son to grow up without a father."

"And he won't have to worry about that. I promise."

Adrian picked up a brush from the table and began brushing Tracey's hair.

Seven walked over and picked up the boy. Tracey giggled, then he said, "Pick me up."

Seven tossed the child up three or four times before taking his seat again.

"Lets say our A-B-C's," Seven said.

"He can count now," Adrian said.

"Oh yeah? This boy is smart as hell."

Adrian said, "One, two . . . come on, baby. Count for Mommy."

Tracey said, "One, two, three, four . . ." Then he looked in the air and started blushing. He had forgotten what comes after four.

Seven said, "Five . . ."

Tracey said, "Six . . . and seven, like Daddy."

Seven smiled. "Seven, like Daddy? What's he talking about?"

"Yeah, that's how I helped him remember seven. Whenever he counts, he says 'seven, like Daddy.'"

Seven smiled. "Little man—you are too much for me to handle." He then picked little Tracey up and stood him up so they faced each other, but the child's legs gave out again and little Tracey started crying. Seven picked up his son. "You know what? It's going to be okay, son. It's going to be okay. Daddy promises." He kissed his son on the head.

CHAPTER 3

he smell of bacon was coming from Elise's kitchen. Seven lay on the futon watching ESPN's SportsCenter.

"Baby, you want something to eat?"

"Is that pork bacon?"

"You know it is, nigga. I'm from the South," Elise said.

Seven looked disgusted. "Now you know I don't fuck with no damn swine, just fix me a fruit salad or something; that swine I cannot fuck with."

Elise took the bacon out of the pan and put three pieces on some bread, then she scooped some scrambled eggs out of a bowl.

"You and your self-righteous bullshit, nigga, I bet your ass was eating bacon before you went to prison. Now, all of a sudden, you can't eat it," she said teasingly.

Seven became angry.

"You don't fucking know me to be telling me what the fuck I was doing before I went in. I don't fuck with no swine. My mama ain't never cook no swine. That's the difference between the North and the South."

"There ain't no difference. People are people."

"Yeah, but people in the North are more conscious about what they eat. Niggas down here just don't give a fuck, they will eat anything. Why da the fuck do you think the black man leads in high blood pressure and heart disease and shit? It's because motherfuckers don't care what they put in their body."

Elise took a bite of her sandwich and walked past him, switching her hips from side to side seductively. "Can you cool it with the fucking preaching?" she said.

Seven's eyes grew. "Goddamn, that ass is fat."

She smiled and said, "Nigga, it's the fuckin' grits and eggs and pork bacon. I bet they ain't got asses like this in New York. Do they?"

"Hell, no," Seven said. Then he thought any man would be weak to that ass. He thought about the nigga that Butter wanted to have robbed. He knew he needed the money to get his son the braces and the operation on his legs. He said, "Baby, I have a plan that will make both of us paid—but I need your help."

"What do you need me to do?"

Seven picked up the remote control from the coffee table and turned the television off.

"I need you to seduce this nigga, find out where he lives, maybe visit him and let me and Butter know. Maybe we can follow you to his house one day."

"Nigga, are you out of your mind?" Elise set her sandwich down. "One thing I'm not is a stupid bitch. I mean, the St. Louis shit was one thing, but putting myself out there in my own city is something else."

Seven looked at her, but didn't respond. He was in deep thought. He hadn't thought that he could possibly be putting Elise's life in danger. All he could think about was his son, and the fact that he needed to be walking.

"Hey, baby. I will never let nothing happen to you." He knew that it was just an empty promise. Just because it sounded good didn't necessarily mean it was the truth; living in the street, he knew that anything could go down at any time.

Elise blushed a little. "I know, but, Seven, I just can't bring myself to do this. Maybe I can find out where he lives, but having you and Butter follow me over there would be too obvious. You know what I mean?"

"Yeah, I feel ya," Seven said, thinking of another way.

■

It was raining money in Club Champagne. Two women wearing G-strings were in the boxing ring, slugging it out. The young thugs threw handfuls of cash into the ring; one guy stood at the side with a trash bag just throwing hundreds of dollar bills into the ring. Adult entertainment at its best on Wednesday night. The club was packed to capacity.

Elise entered with Seven and Butter wearing a form-fitting black dress and heels. She walked past a table of men, who all turned their heads to get a look at the girl with the curvaceous figure. Many of the men even forgot about the strippers.

Reno was the big man at the table with the bucket of champagne. He wasn't a bad-looking guy, but his size made him unattractive. He was so big that he had to sit on two chairs pushed together—but the diamond-crusted cross that he wore made it obvious that he had mad paper. Elise turned and made eye contact with him. He winked at her and she walked over and sat on his lap.

"Baby, you work here?" he asked.

"No, just hanging out with my brothers. You know?" She pointed to Butter and Seven at the bar.

Reno looked at Seven and Butter and waved.

"Can't say y'all look alike. Y'all must not have the same daddy."

"Naw. We all have different daddies, but we love one another; you know?"

"Yes. I know exactly what ya mean. Me and my brothers have different daddies."

A short man from across the table said, "That's the way shit is in the hood."

The big man said, "I'm Reno, and this is my partner, Lil' Chris."

"My name is Lisa," she said quickly, giving him her alias. Elise put her hands on Reno's chest. "So what are you getting into tonight?"

"Nothing really. Chillin' with the fellas, ya know."

"I know that, but I have to get your information before I leave."

Reno frowned. "Where are you going?"

"Back over there with my brothers."

"Tell your brothers to come over here. Everything is on me, if they want champagne, if they want these bitches, I can give them either one of these hos."

"Who are you? Why are you so important?" Elise asked, knowing that she'd heard he had made a million on the streets.

Reno laughed loudly. "I just run shit, ma. You know? I mean, people listen to me."

She rubbed his chest again. "I'm just saying when you have money it makes ya life a whole lot easier." She looked away. "I wouldn't know about that. I've never had money."

Reno smiled. "What yours is mine and what's mine is yours."

Elise put her hand on Reno's dick. She knew he was probably insecure without money, and she was going to make him feel like a king. "Sounds like you're running game on me, big man."

Reno pointed to a trash bag on the floor and told Elise to open it.

Elise untied the knot and was surprised to see the bag was full of money. Her eyes grew.

Reno said, "That's twenty thousand dollars. I'm going to fuck that up right now in the club."

"You're spending twenty thousand dollars on strippers?"

He winked. "Hey. As far as I know you only live once, and I want to make sure I have all the fun I can."

This time Elise put her hands inside his shirt. She felt the hairy rolls on his stomach and chest. *How disgusting*, she thought. But what she said was, "I want to leave with you tonight, Daddy."

Reno smiled. "Is that right?"

■

Reno's uptown penthouse was on the fifty-sixth floor of the Savoy building. The color scheme was basic black. A very manly home, from what she could gather. But before she could check the place out, Reno led her to the bedroom, stripped to his boxers and sat on the king-sized sleigh bed.

Damn, this nigga is disgusting, she thought.

Reno made a motion suggesting that she get next to him.

"No, thank you. I'm fine."

"Come over here and sit down beside me, ma." He smiled. "I don't bite."

She avoided his eyes and tried not to look at his stomach.

"Listen. I don't think I should have come here tonight," she said.

"Why not? I mean, you were talking a lot of shit in the club. I mean, you came on to me. What the fuck is going on?"

"Nothing is going on; it's just I need to go home. I have to work tomorrow."

"Listen. Don't worry about that job. Just chill with me. Call out and I'll pay ya for a week."

She sat on the bed, kind of embarrassed being in the apartment. She felt sort of like a chicken-head. No woman with self-respect would have ever gone to a man's apartment the first night she met him. Her mother had taught her better than that.

She made eye contact with him and decided that he really wasn't *that* bad-looking; he was just a big guy. He had a soft demeanor, which she liked. Maybe he was the kind that grew on you.

Reno stood and put his pants on. “I'm going to put my clothes on because you look a little uncomfortable.”

She smiled. He was so considerate, not like the rest of the young thugs who tried to holla at her. Maybe she should give him a chance.

“So tell me about yourself.”

“What do you want to know?” Elise put a little flirtation into her voice to let him know she was still cool with the situation.

“Were those guys really your brothers?'

She laughed. “Yes. Why would you ask me that?”

“I mean, none of y'all look alike. None of y'all look remotely related. The one guy had an accent like he was from up North or something.”

“You're a very smart man.”

“Where is he from, New York?”

Elise thought about Seven and Butter. They would surely hurt her if she blew their cover, but Reno was nobody's fool. He'd pretty much figured out that they were not related. “You know what? These guys are *like* my brothers. You know?”

Reno nodded his head slowly. “So, did they send you to meet me?”

“What are you talking about?” Elise said, but she knew

exactly what he was asking. She was uncomfortable now because he had called her out.

"Did they put you up on me?"

"Hell, no."

"Just asking cuz, you know, niggas get set up every day by broads."

Elise became irate. "Broads. What do you mean, broads?"

"I'm sorry, but that how I talk. Please don't get offended."

"Not offended. I'm just sayin'—don't refer to me as a broad."

Reno's eyes narrowed. "So why did you pick me? You're a fine-assed woman, can probably have anybody you want. Why did you choose me, Elise?"

She was astounded. She couldn't believe he knew her name. *How did he find out?* she wondered.

"How did you know my name?"

"My boy Ugly-Charles went to Garringer High School with you. He remembers you, says you didn't have any brothers—just sisters."

"Oh, yeah. Lisa is short for Elise, you know."

"Okay; I feel ya. But what about ya boy Butter? Lil' Chris says that nigga is a stick-up kid. Says he robbed his boy, Tom-Tom."

"I don't know nothing about that."

Reno opened his dresser drawer and pulled out a Cuban cigar. He lit the cigar before saying, "He's your brother, and you don't know if he rob?" He sat on the bed. "Well, he's like a brother to you."

"No, I've never heard of him robbing."

Reno showed Elise a watch. "You ever see this watch?"

She recognized the watch immediately. How in the hell did Reno have St. Louis's watch?

"No; I've never seen that before," she lied.

"Bet your brothers have." He laughed. "I gave the niggas thirty grand for this through a third party. That nigga, Butter, said that he'd stuck somebody up for the watch, but you're telling me that they ain't no robbers."

Reno walked over to the window and ordered Elise to come to him. He pointed to the parking deck.

"Do you see those two black G-Wagon trucks?"

"Yeah. What about them?"

"Those are my niggas and they are ready for war." He puffed his cigar again before saying, "I'm going to give you an opportunity to save those niggas' lives, if they *are* up to something. You can call them and tell them not to try no stupid shit."

She giggled, trying to play it off. "I can't believe you would think I would do something like that," she said, thinking about Seven's original plan.

"If it ain't like that, don't worry about it, ma—but if it

is, things will get ugly real fast in this bitch." He looked her dead in her eyes. "I'm a nice guy to most."

"Really, it's not like that," she protested.

"You know what? I like you, I likc you a lot because you didn't slut yourself out for ya boys. And you tell the truth, I get a really good feeling about you. Really, it would be better for them to be my allies than my enemies."

She was totally thrown by that. "Why?"

"Because I make men rich overnight."

Elise smiled in relief. She was happy he liked her, because she knew that a man like him could easily have her killed, and nobody would know.

"So, do you need a ride home?" Reno said, changing the subject.

"Yeah."

"I'll get a driver to take ya home."

She stood back from the window. "So, what ya doing tomorrow?"

"Nothing really. Just handling my business. What's up?"

"Do you want to get some ice cream?"

Reno laughed. No woman had ever asked him out for ice cream before. She was kind of childlike, but he liked that.

"Sure, what time?"

"It doesn't matter to me."

"You're the one with the job, I ain't got shit to do."

"I'll give you a call tomorrow, give me your number."

He told her the digits as she punched them into her phone, then stored it.

“Okay. Just go downstairs to the lobby. I’ll have Ugly-Charles to take ya home. Maybe y’all can do some high school reminiscing.”

■

Ugly-Charles dropped Elise off at her apartment. Seven came over ten minutes later to find her damn near in tears.

“What wrong, baby?”

She looked up at him but didn’t say anything. All she could think of was the fact that Reno could have had them all killed. Her life could have ended at twenty-six.

Seven put his hand underneath her chin. “Baby, what’s wrong with you?”

Still she looked up at him and, finally, she broke down crying. Tears streamed down her pretty face.

He held her close. “Tell me what’s wrong, please. Did that fat motherfucker do something to you? Did he rape you?”

“No, Seven. No!”

“Did he try to take the pussy?” he persisted.

She jerked away from his grip. “No, he didn’t do anything to me, but you did, Seven.”

He was confused. "What did I do?"

"I could have been killed tonight, fucking around with that nigga!"

"What are you talking about?"

"He knew everything. He knew Butter was a robber, he knew you was from New York, and he had a good idea that we were trying to set him up."

Seven's face was without expression. "How did he know this? Who told him?"

"I don't know, Seven. I don't know; but I was so scared, I didn't think I was going to make it out."

"So did you admit to anything?"

"What are you talking about?"

"Did you admit to being a part of a scheme, bitch?"

The word "bitch" infuriated her. She took two steps away from him and then turned her back. "I can't believe what I'm hearing. I cannot *believe* this shit. I mean, I try to help you and you call me a bitch."

He turned her toward him. "I'm sorry, baby. I didn't mean it like that; but I was just wondering did you tell him. I mean—I ain't afraid of nobody, but I just don't want to be walking around looking over my shoulder."

"It ain't like that. I assured him that it wasn't like that. I assured him that there were no plans to rob him."

"Did he believe you?"

"I think so, Seven, but he knows that Butter is a robber. He even had the watch that you and Butter took from St. Louis."

"Are you serious?" Seven couldn't believe this shit. *This city is too damn small*, he thought.

"So how did you convince him that we weren't tryin'a stick him?"

"I guess because there were no signs of you and Butter."

"He was looking for us to follow him?" Seven asked. He couldn't believe this country nigga was actually up on game.

"Yes. He was prepared for you. He had two trucks full of niggas in the parking deck waiting on y'all."

Seven laughed; not because it was funny. He couldn't believe this shit. The nerve of this country-ass nigga preparing to go to war with him. He was furious.

"So where do the nigga live?"

Elise looked at him, dead serious. "Why?"

Seven's eyes narrowed. "What the fuck you mean, why? Because I'ma see that nigga. I'ma to take everything he got."

"Don't do that, Seven. Actually, he can help you."

"What the fuck you mean, he can help me? I don't need his help. I gets."

"You really are a fuckin' idiot." She threw her hands

up, disgusted. "I gave you credit for having far more intelligence than you actually have. The nigga is *major*, and he said that it would better for you and Butter to be his allies than his enemy."

"What did he mean by that?"

"I don't know, but he said something about he could make you rich."

Seven's eyes lit up. "Was he talking about giving us some dope?"

"That's what I was thinking."

Though he had sold weight before, he wondered who he would sell it to now, with no crew and no connects. And besides, he was having a lot of fun robbing.

"You know, I don't know about this."

She looked confused. "Seven, I think I should arrange a meeting."

"Why?"

"I don't see you and Butter continuing to rob much longer. I mean, the streets are already talking, ya know."

"Yeah; I know," Seven said. "You know what? I'm not afraid to admit that you're right."

She smiled. "Good. I will arrange the meeting."

"So—he knows I'm not your brother. Who does he think I am to you?"

"Just a good friend."

“Does he know we’ve fucked?”

She licked her lips. “Doesn’t know we’ve *fucked*, as you put it.”

“Okay. When are you going to see him again?”

“I’m supposed to call him for ice cream tomorrow.”

“Ice cream . . . ? Whose idea was that?”

“It was mine. I had to think of something to do that was innocent, you know.”

“Yeah. I feel ya, I guess.”

CHAPTER 4

Ugly-Charles was tall and skinny, with a wide nose, several moles, and a severe case of unsightly razor bumps. Reno kept him around because he was loyal, and he trusted him with his women because no chick in her right mind would find him attractive. At 5:15 P.M. he picked up Elise in front of her apartment because Reno was running late. He'd just gotten another shipment of coke and needed to make sure it got to his street soldiers.

When Elise hopped into the car, Charles presented her with a gift. A smile covered her face.

"I love presents. What is it, Charles?"

"I don't know. He never tells me these things. I can tell you it's something expensive, though, cuz the nigga has good taste."

Elise figured from Charles's response that Reno bought women gifts all the time. She tore into the package. It was a Louis Vuitton speedy bag.

"I was just telling my sister I wanted one of these, the other day," she squealed. Reno was looking better to her all the time.

■

Charles dropped her off in front Reno's building fifteen minutes later. She met him with a hug, thanked him for the handbag, and they drove to the Häagen-Dazs shop. She ordered a cream deluxe ice cream cone. He passed.

"I'm tryn'a watch my figure," he joked.

She laughed, not because he was amusing, but more to stroke his ego.

"So what's on your mind today?" he asked.

"Nothing," she said, then licked the side of the ice cream cone suggestively.

"Dayum, girl. You are really doing a number on that ice cream."

She blushed. "What you talking about?"

"You gonna get a nigga aroused." He winked.

"I was just thinking about what happened last night and I want you to know that my intentions were never bad."

"I know, or else you wouldn't be sitting here right now but somewhere viewing those two niggas' bodies."

She took her napkin and wiped the side of her mouth. "Damn. Is it that serious?"

"It's that serious out here. I came from nothing. You think I'm 'bout to let somebody take something from me?"

"Nobody wants to take nothing from you, but me and my brothers do need your help."

"Your brothers?"

"Well, my good friends. You know what I mean." She simulated oral sex with the ice cream again.

"The way you licking that ice cream can make me do whatever you want."

She smiled.

He leaned forward and said, "You are sexy as a motherfucker."

She stroked his inner thigh underneath the table. "I know I am."

"What can I help you with?"

"My brothers are looking for a connect."

"A connect? How can I help you with a connect?"

"Come on, man. I know you got it. Don't play dumb."

He stood up and slid into her side of the booth. Then he frisked her, grabbing her breasts and legs.

She laughed. "I'm far from the police, nigga."

"I gotta be safe . . . you understand?" He scooted out of her side of the booth and took his position back on the other side of the table.

"Oh, I understand."

He whispered, "Please don't try me—I think I like you."

She hadn't expected him to say that. She had just seen a different side of him; beneath all that toughness, Reno was a vulnerable human being. "I would never do anything to hurt you," she found herself saying, then she shoved the rest of the ice cream cone down her throat.

■

Seven and Butter met Reno at Club Crush. Reno had a table in VIP. He introduced himself along with Ugly-Charles and Lil' Chris. Charles patted down both of the two men before they sat at the table. "What's that all about?" Seven asked.

"Just checking for wires, homey."

"I feel ya."

Butter and Seven sat directly across from Reno.

Reno took a drink from his champagne glass.

"Butter, I hear your name ringing in the streets. I just want you to know I don't need no unwanted heat my way if we're going to do business."

Butter looked confused. "What're ya saying, man?"

"Nigga, you a stick-up kid. If you gonna to sell dope, sell dope, but none of that robbery shit; especially if you got something that belongs to me."

"One thing I am is a real nigga, and if you help me I can help you. I will leave that shit alone," Butter promised.

Reno said, "Cool."

■

There was half a kilo of coke underneath a white bucket beside a big tree in front of Ugly-Charles's grandma's house. Seven jumped out of the car and scanned the area, looking for police and suspicious characters. Nobody was in sight. He lifted the bucket and grabbed the plastic grocery bag and ran back to the car. Butter pulled off.

■

Back at Butter's house, they weighed the product and bagged it into individual ounces. When they were done they had about seventeen three-quarters. "It's short," Butter announced.

"Yeah, it's a little off," Seven agreed.

"So, what do we do now?"

"Nothing . . . It's only off a quarter. This shit is not worth complaining about. I mean, one thing about this business is you can't be a nickel-and-dime-type nigga; you can't complain about minor shit. I mean, we're about to get some money. Can't be petty."

Butter became angry. "What the fuck do you mean, petty? I mean, I ain't never been no drug dealer like you say you have, but I'm used to having shit, even if I gotta get my shit the ski mask way."

"I didn't say you were petty, I was saying it would be petty of us to complain, you know what I mean?"

"Okay. I just don't need you telling me how to do business, because, I mean, this ain't rocket science."

"It's about being smart, flipping money quick; because once we do that, Reno will build trust in us and we can get more product. More coke—more money. You know?"

"Yeah, I think I know what you mean. I know one cat name Black Kenny. I was gonna rob him, but I'll get in touch with his sister to see if I can get his number," Butter said.

"Cool. Is he major?" Seven wanted to know.

"Naw, but I hear he runs through a lot of coke."

■

Black Kenny was a small, stocky guy and black as a tire. He came to Butter's house with another man that he introduced as his brother.

"So where is the coke?"

Seven showed him an ounce. Kenny opened the bag and tasted it. He looked at his brother and said, "Okay. This is all right." Then he turned and faced Seven. "Aight, I want nine."

"We got plenty, don't worry," Seven bragged, hoping that Black Kenny wasn't a robber or informant. Though this was his first time meeting Kenny, he got a good vibe from him. He seemed to be very business-oriented.

"How much money you asking for?"

"Seventy-two hundred."

"I can give you seven thousand. I mean, it's okay, but it ain't all that," Black Kenny said.

Butter said, "Hell no, nigga. How you gonna set our price?"

Seven pulled him to the side. "Okay, man, I think we should do it. See—what you gotta understand about hustling is the faster the better. If we sell it, we will still make a thousand dollars today."

"I was thinking if we get nine ounces for six, shouldn't we make twelve?"

Seven laughed. He didn't mean to, but it was obvious to him that Butter had never been a hustler.

"We can retail the shit and try to double up or we can cook it and make more, but why do all of that shit when we can make a G with this one transaction and get more product?"

Butter thought hard. "Okay. I think your way makes sense."

Seven said to Black Kenny, "Count your money and it will go down today."

"Cool. I'll be back in about twenty minutes."

■

Seven called Elise and asked her to meet him for lunch.

"I want to, but I have some errands to run," she said.

"Okay. I was wanting to take you out and buy you something really nice because, thanks to you, I'm doing okay for myself," Seven said, thinking about the new car and house that he was now able to afford thanks to the drugs. He thought about Tracey's surgery. He would take care of that in a few weeks. As long as the drugs were available.

"Okay, Seven. Maybe later."

"Can I come over later? You know I miss that ass."

"Naw. I have to work tomorrow."

Seven paused, then said, "I notice we're seeing less and less of each other. What's going on?"

"Nothing is going on . . . just busy, that's all."

"Okay. Maybe we can get together later in the week."

"Maybe." She paused. "I don't know."

"Okay—well, hit me up if you change your mind. Aight?"

"Okay. I will."

Seven thought long and hard after he hung up the phone. Something wasn't right with Elise. He drove to her apartment unannounced. She opened the door wearing some tight jeans and heels, and it looked as if she had just left the hair stylist. She was visibly startled.

"So where are you going?"

"Out with my girlfriend, Candace."

"On a Wednesday?"

"Yes."

"Okay. You'd rather be with that bitch than hang out with me?" Seven asked. He walked into the apartment and scanned the area. He noticed a new Gucci handbag on the kitchen counter.

"So whose bag is this?"

"It's mine."

"Okay. This bag looks expensive. How much?"

She put her hands on her hips. "Why? I don't ever ask you how much shit cost."

"Don't answer the question with a question. How much did the bag cost?"

"Maybe close to two grand."

"What? Who in the hell bought that?"

"Reno bought it."

"Oh. I thought the bag was a Louis Vuitton."

"Yeah, he bought me a Louis, too."

Seven laughed before taking a seat on the sofa. "Oh, I get it. You still seeing that motherfucker."

"He pays the bills."

"What about us?"

"Seven, you don't give a damn about me. All you care about is your damn self. And now that you have the connection, I know you could care less about me."

Seven stood and looked her straight in her eyes. "Now you know that shit ain't true. Girl, I love you."

"Hmph. I don't believe you."

"So, what's the deal? You kicked me to the curb for that fat-assed Reno, huh?"

"Ain't nobody fucking with Reno, nigga. That's all you concerned with anyway, whether I'm fucking another nigga." She went over to kitchen counter and grabbed the bag.

He noticed she was wearing diamond studs.

"Nice earrings you got there. What are those—half a carat?"

"No. A carat, thank you."

"And I guess that nigga bought you those, too."

"What do you think?"

"I think he's your sugar daddy."

Elise walked over to the door and opened it. "I think you should leave now."

"Why?"

"Because I'm about to leave."

Seven walked toward the door. "Oh yeah, I forgot. Candace is coming over."

Elise looked at Seven without saying a word.

CHAPTER 5

Seven stepped into Butter's small apartment and took a seat on the sofa and then said, "I think that bitch Elise is falling in love with Reno."

Butter sat on the chair beside him. "Him, or his money?"

"I don't know, but the nigga is buying her a lot of shit."

Butter asked, "What do you mean?"

"Designer handbags, diamond earrings and shit."

Butter busted open a cigar and sprinkled some weed in it. "Yo. Don't even worry about her, man. We making money. Don't sweat that shit."

"Believe me, I ain't tripping over no bitch, but it's just the principle of it. You know?"

"I mean, the plan was for her to get next to Reno. Right?"

"Yeah, that was the plan."

"Okay. Well, she's done her job, now don't trip."

"I ain't tripping, man."

Butter lit the blunt and then inhaled it. "I mean, you already know Reno is fucking her."

"She says she's not fucking with Reno."

Butter passed the blunt to Seven, but he declined it. "Come on, man, Ugly-Charles is always going to pick her up for Reno."

"So, what does that mean?"

"It means they're going for back massages. Naw; it means he's banging that ass, man."

"Come on. Look at him. The man is totally out of shape," Seven protested.

"But he has money—serious money. Come on, man. You know how that shit works."

Seven didn't say anything. Butter was right. Money was power and a magnet for women.

"Yo. Don't trip, because soon as we get enough bread, man, we can cut this nigga off and get our own connect."

"You're right. We gotta stay focused. Bitches come a dime a dozen. Right?"

"Now that's what I'm talking about."

■

Later that night, Seven followed Elise to PF Chang's. He took a seat in the back of the restaurant, ordered two glasses of Absolut and cranberry juice and was unnoticed. He observed them hugging and kissing. It was obvious that they were a couple now. This was not how his plan was supposed to go. *Damn, she looks great*, he thought. Now she was wearing a backless red Lycra dress. But he was old enough to realize that women always looked great when they were with somebody new. He couldn't believe that he was actually jealous. He very rarely got jealous. He had always manipulated women. Never would he let a country bitch manipulate him!

The waitress brought out a birthday cake, and the whole staff sang "Happy Birthday" to Reno. After that, he saw Elise pull out a gift and hand it to Reno. He opened the package. Seven heard one of the waitresses say: "Cartier. She must love you a lot."

Reno tongue-kissed Elise.

Seven fumed under his breath. He flagged the waitress, ordered two more drinks and was soon buzzing.

After they left PF Chang's, they headed to Reno's place. After going to the store to get some Heineken, Seven parked across the street and waited for her to come out. He figured that Ugly-Charles would take her home. He waited, and he waited, and he waited. Finally, Ugly-Charles arrived at four in the morning. Elise ran out and jumped in the car with Charles. Seventeen minutes later she entered her apartment. When Charles was out of sight, Seven knocked on the door.

"Yeah; who is it?"

"Seven."

"Yeah; what do you want?"

"I want to talk."

"Can we talk later?"

"No. I want to talk now."

"Seven, please leave."

"I will not leave . . . in fact, if you don't open this damn door, I'm going to make a scene out here."

She opened the door. He walked into the apartment.

"Okay, Seven, what's so damn important that you had to come in here at four in the morning?" Elise fumed.

"Oh, I know you were awake."

"What the hell is that supposed to mean?"

"You still have your dress on. Did ya change clothes to meet Candace?" He pointed to her feet. "And stilettos. So don't tell me you were sleep."

She put her hands on her hips, frustrated. "Okay, what is that supposed to mean?"

"Means you were out with the fucking birthday boy," he slurred.

She could smell the alcohol on his breath.

"Okay, yeah, I was out."

Seven grabbed her hand. "So do you love this nigga?"

She pulled away from him and didn't answer his question.

"So, it's like that, Ms. Rich Bitch? You're too good for small-time hustler Seven?"

"I don't know what you're talking about."

He stood in front of her again. "I'm talking about our plans."

She fanned his breath, then offered him a piece of gum.

He knocked it out of her hand. "I don't need no gum from you . . . I don't need shit from you, bitch."

She walked over toward the door and opened it. "Seven, I think you should go."

He stepped past her and closed the door. "That why I don't trust women, cuz of bitches like you hood-rat hos!"

"Nigga, who the fuck you calling a hood rat?" she screamed.

"You!" he yelled back.

"Get the fuck out of my house!"

"I ain't got to go nowhere."

"Oh, you leaving, or else I'm calling the police."

"Oh, you're a snitch. You fucking with the biggest dope dealer in this little country-assed city and you have the nerve to be a snitch."

He leaned toward her and said, "All I wanted to do was to make sure we're okay, baby. That's the reason I wanted to rob Reno in the first place. All I ever did was for the team." A tear came down his face. "You and my little man is the only two people I have to worry about. Did I tell you my son can't walk?"

She didn't say anything.

He pulled out a picture of little Tracey.

"Seven, you're incoherent. You're not making any sense."

"I know exactly what I'm saying." He showed her the picture.

"Seven, I've seen your son before. Remember?" Elise tried to hide her impatience, but she wanted to get this drunk fool out of her house—now.

He kissed the picture. "He's all I got in the world . . . I don't give a fuck about you, bitch . . . you know why?"

"What are you talking about?"

He grabbed her hands and pinned her to the wall. "You didn't stick to the plan."

"Seven, let me go or I'm going to scream."

He lowered his voice. "The plan wasn't for you to fall in love with this nigga. The plan was for us to blow up together."

"If I remember the plan correctly, I think the plan was for you and Butter to rob Reno," she said sarcastically.

He kissed her roughly, sticking his tongue down her throat. "I love you. Can't you see I love you?"

She pushed him back, then ran and got the cordless telephone from the kitchen counter. "I'm calling the police."

Seven grabbed her by her throat and started choking her. She gasped for air.

"Stop! I can't . . . breathe . . ."

"You don't deserve to breathe, bitch."

She grabbed his testicles; he released her, then kicked her in her stomach and punched her in the eye. Elise fell to the floor.

Seven grabbed her cell phone and stomped on it. Then he grabbed the cordless and slammed it on the floor.

■

"I punched that bitch in her face," Seven told Butter over his cell. It was five in the morning and Seven was driving home.

"Nigga, why you do some stupid shit like that? Now you know the bitch is going to call the police on you."

"I don't give a fuck."

"I can't believe you were so stupid."

"The bitch disrespected me!" Seven shouted.

"Well, you know that that nigga Reno is going to hear about that."

"I don't give a fuck. I'm ready to go to war. I don't give a damn about no connection and I damn sure don't give a fuck about no bitch."

"Well, dawg, you know I'm with you, but I have to say that was some foul shit, man."

"All the bitch had to do was just play her position."

Butter yawned and then said, "Seven, you were out of line, man."

"What the fuck you mean *I* was out of line? You on her side or something?"

"No; but you just let your emotions get the best of you. Now it's going to be bad for everybody."

"I don't give a fuck."

"You just better hope that bitch don't call the police and take out a warrant on your ass. I mean, you probably fucked up her face."

"That was my intention."

"Seven . . . go home, man. Get you some rest. You definitely don't need to be driving drunk."

"I ain't drunk. I only had a couple of drinks."

"Go home. I will talk to you tomorrow, but—yeah, get some sleep."

■

Butter knocked on Seven's door at two in the afternoon. Seven opened the door wearing nothing but his boxer shorts.

"Hey, nigga. Are you still sleeping?"

"My head is killing me," Seven said, groaning.

"You was tripping last night."

"What do you mean?'

"I mean you called me and told me you punched Elise in the face."

Seven looked surprised. The last thing he remembered was following Elise and Reno to PF Chang's.

"Was I joking? Did I say that I wanted to punch her in her face, or did I say that I punched her in the face?"

"You said that you punched her in the face."

"I don't remember that." Seven picked up his cell phone, which was lying on the kitchen counter, and dialed Elise's number.

"Don't you ever call my phone again, you black mother-fucker!" she screeched.

"What are you talking about?" Seven winced; her voice drove through his skull like an ice pick.

"I'm talking about you're going to regret the day you laid hands on me, motherfucker!"

"Hey, if I hit you I'm sorry, but I don't remember nothing."

"Fuck you, Seven."

"Calm down and talk to me. What happened."

"Nigga, you know damn well what happened. You were there."

"Can we meet?"

"Hell no! We can't meet nowhere. I don't want to see you. I don't want to see nobody. My eye is fucked up."

"Elise, I'm sorry. I've never hit a woman in my life. I have sisters, and a mother—"

"I don't give a damn about your sister or your ho-ass mama."

"You're out of line now."

"Fuck you." She terminated the call.

■

Reno opened the door and let Elise into his apartment. She took off her sunglasses.

"What happened to your eye?"

"Seven did it."

Reno was confused. "What? Were you playing or something?"

"No. He meant to do it."

"Why did he punch you?"

She put her glasses back on to avoid looking at him.

"Come on . . . why did he hit you?"

"He hit me because I'm with you now."

"Why doesn't he want us together?"

She laid her head on his chest. "I don't want you to be mad at me."

He stepped away from her. "Now why would I be mad at you?"

She started crying a little.

"Okay, now I'm starting to understand. He means something to you; more than your so-called brother, huh?"

"Yes. We were close, once," she said softly.

"What happened?"

"I'm going to be honest with you . . . even if you hate me later. I have to tell the truth."

Reno sat down on the sofa. "I don't like the sounds of this already."

"Well, Reno, the night I met you in the club, I was told to holla at you by Seven and Butter."

"They were tying to get connected?"

"No, they wanted to rob you."

He put his hand underneath his chin. "Just as I thought. Those niggas were up to no good."

"Exactly."

"But you were up to no good too."

She sat beside Reno but he stood and walked away.

"You were going to set me up. Just as I thought."

"No, I was just supposed to find out where you live."

"That's the same fucking thing. What are you, out of your mind?"

She was silent for a moment, and then she couldn't hold back her tears. "I'm sorry. Really, I am."

"I think you should get the fuck out of my house before I punch you in your other eye."

She took a step toward him but he pushed her back. She kept coming. Finally, she grabbed his hands and placed her head back on his chest.

"Reno, I love you."

"Do you love me or my money?"

"I love you. I have to admit I didn't always love you, but I've grown to love you." She kissed him. He tried to push her off but finally he gave in.

Five minutes later his boxers were down to his ankles and she was on her knees with his sex in her mouth. He was weak for her—he couldn't help himself. She made him feel so good. He looked at her licking up and down his shaft, the saliva dripping; she made the head job so intense. Damn he wished it could last forever! He grabbed the back of her head and started humping her face.

After he came to an orgasm, he said, "So tell me—if Seven hadn't put his hands on you, would you have told me about his plan?"

"I don't know. Maybe, eventually."

"I'm going to hurt those niggas."

"Please don't. I don't want to be in the middle of no shit."

"It's a little too late for that."

"I know," she said softly.

"I'm not going to physically hurt them, just going to cut them off."

"Oh. Okay."

"Cutting their resources will hurt them more, you see. They done got used to making money now."

■

Seven called Ugly-Charles and told him that he needed more product.

Charles responded, "It's not going to happen."

"What do you mean, it's not going to happen?"

"The boss said we won't be fucking with y'all cats no more."

"What about the five grand I owe you?"

"Keep it. It's peanuts."

"I'm not understanding," Seven said. Then he realized he'd been cut off for punching Elise in the face. "This has something to do with that bitch. Right?"

"Listen, man, I ain't got shit to do with this. I'm just following orders."

"Put your boss on the phone."

"Yeah, this is Reno."

"What's up, man? Why can't we do good business?"

"Nigga—you are a robber. You lucky we don't bury your punk ass."

"Oh, no. Now you got shit twisted, playboy. You ain't dealing with a coward."

"Nigga, my nine millimeter will have your body looking like Swiss cheese."

"Oh, after they made one gun, they didn't stop making them."

"So what you saying, nigga?"

"I'm saying don't make threats unless you ain't scared to die."

"If I see you in the streets, it's on."

"Fuck you, fat bastard." Seven terminated the call. He called Butter, who picked up on the second ring.

"What's the business?"

"We've been cut off."

"Seen that one coming."

"The bitch told Reno that we were planning on robbing him."

"Can't trust women, man. You know they talk."

"So what's the plan?"

"I don't know, man. The only niggas that I know we sell to . . . they can't be our connect because we were theirs."

"Shit. We might have to make a trip to New York. My cousin knows some Dominicans we can cop from. I can holla at that nigga and we can go uptown and get at least a half a brick for about nine thousand."

"Sounds like a plan to me."

CHAPTER 6

even's aunt Angie lived in a modest home in Jamaica, Queens. She opened the door and greeted him with a big hug. She shook Butter's hand.

"Where is Antonio?" Seven asked.

She looked surprised. "In the back room." She yelled out, "Tony, your cousin Seven is here. Come out."

Tony appeared. He was shabbily dressed, his eyes were red and he reeked of marijuana smoke. "What's up, nigga? Been a long time."

"Yeah, you know I caught that bid down South." Seven hugged his cousin and then said, "This is my man, Butter."

"Yeah, I know. I was talking to your brother Andre about you the other day. He said he hadn't heard from you."

Seven looked serious. "You know I don't fuck with nobody in the family, man. They kind of left me out to dry when I was down. No money, no letters, no visits—nothing."

"Yeah, I know how that shit is. I was up in Elmira myself

and nobody come to see me, either. Not even that stinking-assed baby mama of mine."

"So, what's up?"

"Come back to the room," Tony said. When they entered, the first thing Seven saw was a large keyboard, and that the place was littered with hip-hop magazines. "Nigga, I see you still into hip-hop."

"Yeah, man. I'm recording a demo next week. I just got to make some money to get some tracks from this up-and-coming producer."

Seven wanted to laugh at his cousin. The man was thirty-two years old, an age where most rappers retire, and he had yet to make it; but he still had hopes of becoming a hip-hop star. Antonio refused to give up on his dream. "I need to make money too, Antonio."

Antonio lit a blunt and passed it to Seven. "So what's the plan?"

Seven hit the blunt. "I need coke, man."

Antonio looked at Seven like he was crazy. "What? Nigga, you still fucking around with that shit?"

"Yeah, man. Me and my man Butter got it crackin' down South."

"So, what? You need a plug or something?"

"Yeah, man. Do you still fuck with Flako 'n' 'em uptown?"

"Naw, man, Flako went to jail, but his man, Premo, is

doing the shit now. But I don't fuck around uptown. I mean, every now and then I'll go get some bud or something, but you know my hustling days are over."

"Why ain't ya trying to get no money?" Seven asked.

"Too old for a bid, man. I mean, I did time when I was younger, but now I can't do it."

Nigga's too old to go to prison, but not to old to have aspirations to be a rapper, Seven thought.

"So can you help us?" Butter asked.

"I mean, I can make some phone calls and shit." Antonio puffed the blunt, then he turned to Seven. "Nigga, you used to know motherfuckers uptown too."

"Man, I've been gone. Shit has changed, you know."

"Aight. What am I going to get out of the deal?" Antonio said.

"Depends," Seven said.

"On what?"

"On how much the price of the shit is."

"Nigga, you know how those Spanish mufuckas is. Man, they price that shit by the gram."

Seven laughed. "Yo. Those niggas still running round with the little calculator watches and shit?"

"Some of 'em. Them niggas is serious about the bread."

Seven looked serious. "I'm relentless about mine too, nigga."

"Give me a G and I can get my boy Squeeze from Harlem to holla at his peeps."

"Lil 'short nigga with a razor mark across his neck?" Seven wanted to know.

"Naw, this Squeeze is tall. I met the nigga on the Island."

"Okay. Call 'em and see what's poppin'."

"Let me hold your cell phone."

Seven passed Antonio the cell phone and he called. Squeeze picked up on the second ring. "Speak your piece."

"Yo, this Tonio from Queens, nigga. What's up?"

"What the fuck you doing calling me from a South Carolina number?"

"North Carolina."

"Whatever. Both of 'em is country as hell."

"Yeah, my cousin Seven is up here and he's tryin'a get down and dirty. Feel me?"

"Yeah. Watch what you say over my horn, nigga."

"I understand. Can you help us?"

"I don't know. I'll call Premo."

"Hit him and call me back."

Thirty minutes and two blunts later Seven's phone rang. It was Squeeze. He passed it to Tony. "Yo, what up?"

"Yeah, my man is good."

"What's the ticket?"

"Like sixteen."

Antonio whispered to Seven, "It's sixteen dollars a gram."

"Okay I need a half a brick," Seven replied.

"Yo. Me and my cousin will meet up with you," Tony said to Squeeze. "What's a good spot?"

"Meet me at Manna's on 125th."

"Okay. We'll be there in an hour."

■

Squeeze was chomping on collard greens and ribs when they approached his table. He stood, wiped his mouth with a napkin and shook hands with Antonio.

"Hey, this is my cousin Seven and his friend, Butter," Antonio said.

"What's good?" Squeeze said. "Y'all niggas from down South?"

Seven looked at him oddly. He knew that a lot of New York cats were looking to prey on dudes from the South. He quickly answered, "I'm from Queens. Why?"

Squeeze smiled "No reason, just asking. It's not where you from, it's where you at, son."

"Naw. I'm just getting money down South but you know I'm from here."

Squeeze sat down, made the others wait while he finished

his ribs and paid the tab. His Lexus truck was parked outside on Frederick Douglass Boulevard. "Hop in, but wipe your feet. I don't have floor mats and I just cleaned this piece. You know what I mean?"

Antonio sat in the front, Butter and Seven sat in the back. Squeeze put in a G-Unit mix tape and pulled off in a hurry as they bobbed their heads to the latest Lloyd Banks song. "Yo, that nigga Banks is nice. I like his delivery," Squeeze said.

"Yeah, but I think Tony Yayo is the nicest," Antonio said.

"Hell, that nigga Fifty is the nicest to me. I mean, this nigga is getting his marbles. They can hate if they want, but he has an empire—clothes, music, video games, Vitamin Water . . ." Seven said.

"Yeah. That's what the fuck I'm talking about; making that dough, man."

Squeeze turned the volume down in the car. "So, y'all niggas tryin'to get a half a brick, huh?"

"Yeah," Seven said.

"How much paper you got?"

"We go eight Gs. Well, nine, including the money we got for you," Seven lied. He didn't want him to know that he had eleven grand. Though he'd been gone from New York, he knew city niggas could be grimy.

"Okay. That should work." Squeeze dialed out on his cell phone. "I will be there in thirty minutes," he said into the phone, then he turned the music up. Fifteen minutes later he pulled into some housing projects, hit the child locks, pulled out a gun and pointed it at Tony.

"What the fuck is going on?" Tony screamed.

"Give me your wallet, nigga."

Seven tried to open the door, but it was locked.

Squeeze pointed the gun at Butter. "Nigga, if you move I will fucking blow your block off."

Butter put his hands up. "Listen, man, I don't need no problems."

"Give me your money, nigga; both of y'all."

Seven gave him the small amount of money he'd had in his front pocket and some change.

Squeeze threw the coins back in Seven's face.

Tony had his face covered, shaking. "Please, cuz. Give him the money before he hurts us."

"Yeah, motherfucker. Where is the money?"

"Give him the money, Butter."

Butter dug into his boxers to get the money and Squeeze put the gun up to his head. "Strip, nigga, but no funny stuff. If I see a gun, I'm killing you, nigga." His eyes were serious.

"I don't have a gun," Butter said.

"Let me get that money, nigga."

Butter gave him the small pouch with the money in it.

"Come on. Let us go. Don't hurt us, man," Antonio said.

Seven looked at Butter. "I can't believe this shit."

"Believe it, niggas. You've been had NYC style. Now get the fuck out my car."

Squeeze unlocked the doors. "I'm going to count to three. If you ain't out of my car, I'ma blow a hole in your back."

The three men exited the car quickly. Squeeze pulled off in a hurry.

■

The men caught a taxi back at the Hilton on Sixth Avenue with $20 Tony had in his sock. Butter got his gun from his suitcase. "I told you we should have brought the tool."

"I thought my cousin was going to hook us up with good people." Seven glanced at Tony.

"I didn't think the nigga was going to pull no slick shit," Tony protested.

"Sorry ain't going to bring our paper back," Butter said angrily.

Seven thought about his son and how he needed his operation; how he depended on his daddy. He then looked at his cuz. "Nigga, I believe you had something to do with this bullshit."

"I was going to say something, but I know he's your cousin," Butter said.

"I swear to you, cuz, I didn't think he was going to pull that shit; you know?"

"The shit just didn't seem right," Seven said. Squeeze had been more concerned with him and Butter. Seven grabbed the gun from Butter and cocked the hammer.

"Antonio, don't lie to me, man. What the fuck just happened?'

Tony began to sweat. "I don't know what went on. Honestly."

"Nigga, this was your friend," Butter said.

"I ain't going to take no motherfucking loss," Seven said. He lowered the gun and then walked around the room.

"We blood, man. You know I wouldn't dare do you like this," Tony pleaded.

Seven's face became really serious. "How do you know this man?"

"I met him on the I-Island," Tony stuttered. "I think it was around '98 or '99, when I caught my second bid."

"Okay. Now it's 2006. You've been knowing him for seven years. Where the fuck does he live?" Seven demanded.

"I don't know. I don't know. All I know is that he's from Harlem and he's in Washington Heights a lot."

"Does he have a baby mama?" Butter asked suddenly.

"I don't know. Why?"

"Nigga, cuz if we can't get to him, we'll kidnap his baby

mama." Butter got angry and backhanded Tony. "You ain't dealing with no coward-ass niggas."

Seven thought hard. "Oh yeah. Your man was really concerned about where we from. Why?"

"I don't know."

Butter punched Tony in the face and blood shot from his nose.

Tony held his nose. "Come on, cuz. Do your really think I had something to do with it?"

"I don't know what to believe."

"I know you had something to do with it," Butter said.

Tony looked at Butter. "I'm really tired of you."

Butter pushed him, and Tony turned and charged Butter, knocking him onto the bed. Seven put the gun up to Tony's head. "Nigga, ease up or I will blast your bitch ass."

Tony held his hands up. "So you're going to take this nigga's side."

Seven smacked him in the face with the gun. "Motherfucker, I'm out eleven thousand dollars because of you."

Tony fell to the bed, holding his face. "Cuz—I'm telling you, I didn't have anything to do with it." His face was still bleeding.

Butter opened the closet and got the iron and put the plug in the socket.

Tony looked scared. "What is this nigga about to do?"

"Nigga, tell us where Squeeze lives and you won't have no problems," Butter said calmly.

"I don't know where he lives."

"Nigga, tell us where he lives or I'm burning you with the fucking iron," Butter said.

"Come on, cuz, don't let him do this to me," Tony pleaded.

"Tell us where he lives," Seven repeated.

Butter unplugged the iron and walked toward Tony, who was still lying on the bed.

"Come on, man, don't do this."

"Nigga, I'm burning your face if you don't tell me where the goddamned money is," Butter said.

"How'm I supposed to know where the money is?"

Butter put the iron inches away from Tony's face. "You better tell me something."

"I don't know shit."

"You gonna side with a nigga that don't give a fuck about you," Seven said.

Butter pressed the iron on Tony's hand.

"Oh shit!" Tony screamed. "Give me the phone. I'll see if I can reach him."

Seven gave Tony the phone. He dialed the number, but the call went straight to voice mail.

"Call again or somebody going to find you dead and stankin'," Butter said.

Tony dialed another number. A female answered the phone. He screamed, "Ma, if anything happens to me I'm with Seven."

Seven yanked the phone out of his hand and terminated the call. "Nigga, you're a real slick motherfucker. That might have saved you from getting killed but it ain't gonna save your ass from getting burned with this hot-assed iron."

Seven held his arms while Butter pressed the iron to the side of Tony's face, his skin melting away.

CHAPTER 7

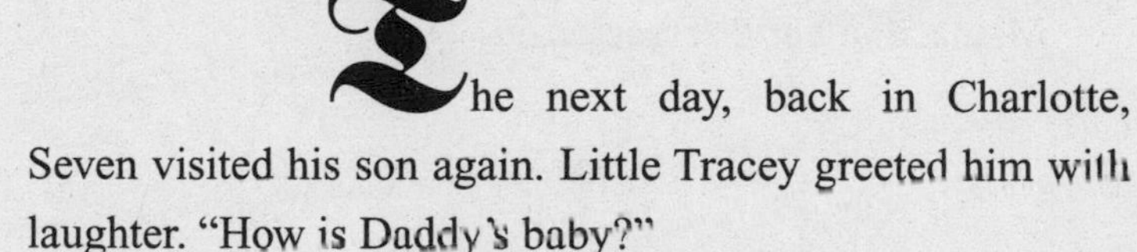

he next day, back in Charlotte, Seven visited his son again. Little Tracey greeted him with laughter. “How is Daddy’s baby?”

“I’m doing great, Daddy.” Tracey smiled.

Seven was impressed that the boy was learning words fast. He turned to Adrian. “This boy is going to be really smart.”

“I’m telling you, it’s Barney. All he does is sit in front of the television all day and watch Barney.”

Seven fell silent. He was happy his boy was learning fast, but he still wanted him to be active. Now he knew that he had very little money and no connection. He knew he would have to start over. He would have to rob again.

“What’s the status with the braces?”

“You know, I signed up for Medicaid and I think they’re going get the braces for us.”

“That’s great,” Seven said.

"That's great, Daddy," Tracey said.

"No, it's not great. I mean, I'm thankful for the braces, but there's still the matter of therapy. And I want him to have the operation to straighten his legs out, because when he plays with kids they don't understand why he can't walk, and he wants to walk," Adrian said. A tear trickled down her cheek. "He tries so hard, you know?"

"Yeah, I know."

"Mama, don't cry," Tracey said.

■

Seven poured some orange juice into the glass of vodka and stirred. He passed the glass to Butter. They sat at the kitchen table of Seven's apartment.

"So what's the plan?" Seven asked.

Butter sipped the liquor. "I don't know, but I know we gotta get somebody my bills, and shit is piling up."

"I feel ya," Seven said. He opened his wallet. There were four one-hundred-dollar bills and two twenties. "My rent is due next week."

"First why don't ya call that bitch back and apologize. Maybe she can tell the nigga she lied cuz she was emotional and shit," Butter suggested.

"Fuck that, man. That nigga threatened me, and I don't

know how y'all get down in the South, but where I'm from, if a nigga threatens you, it's on."

"Oh, I understand. But shit is bad for us now, man. Sometimes you gotta swallow your pride."

"I ain't swallowing shit."

"I'm with you, playboy."

"I was thinking of apologizing to the bitch only because I've never hit a woman before, and I could use her help to put us up on more licks."

Butter looked at Seven like he was an idiot. "She don't need to do licks no more. She fucking with a nigga that's got birds. Remember?"

"Yeah, I know. We'll figure something out," Seven said. He drank his glass of vodka straight.

■

Black Kenny wore a Scarface T-shirt when he met Seven and Butter at the car wash. He was parked in a bay when they drove up. He had nine thousand dollars in a knockoff Gucci book bag. When he opened it and Butter saw the money, Seven pressed the gun to Kenny's temple. "Run it, nigga."

Kenny started shaking. "What the fuck is going on?"

"I need that paper," Butter said. He then snatched the bag from Kenny's hand.

"Come on, Butter. Man, why does it have to be this way?" Kenny said.

"Put your hands up where I can see them," Seven said.

Kenny eased his hands up. "I thought we were doing good business, man. I've spent thousands of dollars with y'all, and this is the thanks I get?"

Seven pointed the gun between Kenny's eyes, letting him see down the barrel.

"Come on, man, please don't kill me."

"Where the fuck is that bitch-ass brother of yours?" Butter said.

"I don't know," Kenny said.

"Nigga, what ya got at your house?" Seven asked.

Kenny turned to Butter. "Man, you know I still live with my grandma."

Butter slapped him in the mouth. "Ghetto-assed motherfucker. You out here making money still living with Grandma? What kind of shit is that?"

Kenny was confused. "Butter, why you robbing *me*? I've been knowing you since I was fifteen. Now what kind of shit is that?"

"Nigga, I'm hungry out here and you got what I want, so give it up," Butter replied simply.

"I've given you everything I have."

"Where the jewels at?"

"I ain't got no jewels."

"Give me what's in your pocket."

Kenny dug into his pocket and pulled out seven hundred-dollar bills. He passed them to Butter.

Seven put the gun to Kenny's head. "Strip, nigga."

Butter said, "Take off everything except your boxer shorts and get the fuck out of here."

Kenny pulled his pants down.

Seven ripped the Scarface T-shirt. "Now get the fuck outa here, nigga, before I blast your ass."

As Kenny got out of the car, Seven kept the gun pointed at him and got out too. He went to Kenny's Dodge Charger and locked all the doors, then got back in the car with Butter and they screeched off, laughing.

■

Butter was driving down Freedom Drive when Seven yelled, "Stop the car!"

Butter turned the music down and looked at Seven oddly. "What's wrong?"

"There's that bitch, Elise, over there at the ATM."

Butter looked at the teller. "Yeah. That's her, all right."

"Pull the car over there."

"Nigga, have you forgotten we just robbed Kenny?"

"I know. But I have to let this bitch know how I feel."

Butter pulled the car behind Elise. Seven hopped out the car. Elise was startled when she saw him.

"What do you want?"

"I just want to talk, that's all."

"I don't want to talk to you."

"First off, I apologize for what I did at your house, but you are out of line."

"Nigga, you got some nerve to tell me I'm out of line."

"Elise, do you love the nigga?"

"What do you mean?"

Seven looked her directly in her eye. "I'm just curious. Do you love Reno?"

"What's it to you?"

"I mean I thought me and you were vibing, but it's like you sold out for a few dollars."

"Nigga, you were using me, so what are you talking about?"

"I'm talking about me and you." Seven's eyes became serious.

"Me and you . . . there is no me and you."

He grabbed her hand. "I love you, and I don't want to see you with anybody else."

She snatched her hand back and took a deep breath. "Seven, please leave me alone."

"I mean, Elise—is money that important that you can just drop everything we have and move on like that?"

"Seven, you were playing the game and I was playing the game. Don't you see there is no us?"

"There is no us?"

"Seven, I didn't love you, and if you really think about it, you didn't love me."

"So, do you love Reno?" he demanded.

"I'm not going to answer that," she replied.

"I don't think ya love him."

"Seven, you don't know shit about me."

"I thought we were a team. You know, like Bonnie and Clyde."

"Nigga, you been watching too much TV."

He grabbed her hand again and held it for a few seconds, then kissed it and let her go. "I love you, and I felt you was the one chick I could possibly marry." Seven knew from experience that most women wanted to get married. Whether they were strippers, whores or doctors, the idea of marriage had been embedded in them since they were little girls.

She looked at him for a long time, and then she said, "Seven, don't give me the bullshit." She walked over to her car—a Benz—and sped off.

■

Butter was wheeling the Impala, and Seven had the seat all the way back, almost lying flat. He gazed at the sky. It was pitch-black dark now and they were about to turn in. Butter put in a screwed-up mix CD. UGK was playing.

"You know I miss that bitch," Seven said.

"Who?"

"Elise, nigga."

Butter turned the radio down. "She dirty, man—this is the same chick that told Reno about the plan to hit him up."

"Yeah, I know, but I think it was my fault, man. I shouldn't have put my hands on her."

Butter laughed. "You getting soft?"

"Nah, just getting older."

"Nigga, you're getting soft. Have you forgotten this chick is sexing the three-hundred-pound nigga? She nothing but a ho."

The word "ho" infuriated Seven but he wouldn't let Butter get under his skin. He didn't say anything. He just thought about Elise and how everything unfolded with her. He was glad he'd seen her today and he knew that he would think about her for the rest of the night.

"Do you love her?" Butter asked.

Seven ignored the question and laughed.

"Do you love her, nigga?"

Seven looked at Butter, then back at the stars in the sky and finally uttered, "I think I do."

■

Seven was alone in his small room with the ski mask and his $4,500 from robbing Black Kenny laid on the bed. He counted the money again. Damn, he'd become really petty, he thought. He remembered the crew in Richmond. Nights of free-flowing champagne, European automobiles and the hordes of beautiful women that came with being a successful hustler. *Damn, those were the days,* he thought. He picked up a picture from the dresser. He stood in front of his 600 Benz. It was all white. Stanley Trill Johnson had gotten the black one. He'd always remember the day they drove the cars off the lot. He missed that lifestyle. He missed his crew. What would they think of him now? They'd despised robbers, especially small-time stick-up kids. Forty-five hundred dollars. There were nights where he'd spent this in the strip club. Though he hadn't used the ski mask to rob Black Kenny it had become a way of life for him. But what else was he to do? He couldn't get a job because he was a felon. Even if he was to get a job, there was no way he could support himself and his son.

He put the mask on and picked up his gun, cocked the hammer and pointed it as his reflection in the mirror over the dresser. “I want everybody to lay the fuck down or else it’s on.” He laughed a loud wicked laugh. Then he whispered, “What have I become . . . what have I become?” He took the mask off and sat on the edge of the bed, looked at the picture again. A tear trickled down his cheek.

CHAPTER 8

Elise looked at her new plasma television in her new high-rise apartment. She couldn't believe her life had changed so drastically over the past few months. Here she was, a girl from the hood, who now had everything money could buy—a Benz, a high-rise apartment, designer clothes and bags. Reno cared a lot about her and she knew it, but the problem was he cared about a lot of other women, too. Last week she'd gotten the code to his cell phone and checked his messages. There were women calling from as far away as Seattle, Washington, thanking him for their rent money. So, Reno loved everybody and everybody loved Reno. She started to confront him about it but decided not to because she was living better than she'd ever lived in her entire life—but she wasn't happy. She was happier when she was with Seven and they didn't have anything. She had been glad to see him today. Damn, he still looked good. She thought about what he'd said about her becoming his wife. The thought brought tears to her eyes. She picked up her cell phone, scrolled to his number, then called. He picked up on the second ring.

"Hello."

"Hey."

Seconds went by with neither one of them saying anything. Finally, he said, "You are still fine as a mother-fucker."

She laughed. "So, did you think I would fall off?"

"No. Never that."

"Seven, you were looking good, yourself."

A long pause, and then he asked, "Is he making you happy?"

"Let's not talk about him," she said quickly.

"What do you want to talk about?"

"I kind of need some . . . you know."

He laughed. "The motherfucker has money but he can't lay the pipe, huh?"

"Come on, Seven. Man, you're ruining my mood. I don't wanna talk about him."

"So, you want me to come over?"

"Yeah. I live downtown now, in the Ivey building."

"Damn. What a come-up."

"Come on over, Seven. I'll be waiting."

■

When Elise opened the door she was wearing a little red teddy she'd gotten from Victoria's Secret. Seven picked her up and carried her to the sofa. He peeled off the teddy and started feasting on her pussy. She was moaning with anticipation, kept pushing his head between her thighs. She screamed, "Put it in, nigga!"

Seven grabbed her legs, spread them wide and thrust deeply, and they kissed. At that moment she realized how much she had really missed him. After the sex was over, tears were coming down her face. He was surprised when she said, "Seven, I'll do anything for you."

"I don't want you to do anything for me, I just want you to be with me."

She looked into his eyes. "I know his whole operation."

"What are you talking about?"

"Reno, he has a Houston connection. He's getting about fifty kilos a week."

"Fifty? Damn. That's serious."

"It comes in on Wed—"

He kissed her lips, silencing her. "So, why are you telling me this?"

She looked away.

"Why are you telling me this," he repeated, "and how can I be sure this ain't a setup?"

"I don't know. I kind of felt bad for letting him know what we'd planned together. But when you put your hands on me, I just lost it, you know?"

"You know I was drunk. I would never hurt you—never. I don't hit women."

She grabbed his dick. "So, can I have some more?"

"You miss me, don't you?"

"You already know I miss you."

"Yeah." He kissed her again. Then he asked, "You say the work comes in on Wednesdays?"

"Yeah."

"You know I ain't got shit. Right? I need this lick badly."

"Seven, not only will you be able to get the work, but you'll be able to get the money too. I'll let you know where the connect is."

"You'll do that for me?"

"I'll do anything for you. I just want to be with you."

"Oh yeah?"

"Yeah."

He kissed her again. Five minutes later they were on the sofa again, feeling each other's love.

■

Butter and Seven were playing with Tracey.

"Give him five, Tracey," Butter ordered.

Tracey smacked Seven's hand.

"My son is smart as hell too. The lil 'nigga can count to twenty now and say his A-B-C's, you know," Seven said proudly.

"Damn. That's some real shit," Butter said.

"I know. I just wish he could walk."

Adrian walked into the room after eavesdropping on the conversation. "Got bad news about the braces."

Seven looked at her. "What do you mean, bad news?"

"Just got turned down for Medicaid."

"Why?"

"Said I wasn't eligible. They say I make too much money." She threw her arms up in disgust. "Can you believe that shit?" Then the phone rang in the kitchen and she exited the room.

Butter looked at Seven. "Why don't you buy the braces, nigga, you've had the money . . . quit being so damn petty."

"The braces ain't the only problem. The main problem is the physical therapy and the surgery. They're going to have to break his legs and straighten them out," Seven explained.

"Damn . . . that's some serious shit."

"I know, and some expensive shit. That's why we gotta get busy."

Butter looked at Seven. "You got a plan?"

"You bet I got a plan; a plan like you've never seen in your life."

"Now that's what the fuck I'm talking about."

"Yeah, the nigga gets the work in on Wednesday."

"Who?"

"Reno."

"How'd you find that out?"

"Elise told me."

Butter looked at him oddly. "You fucking with that bitch again?"

Seven frowned. "Man, don't you see my son in here?"

"Yeah . . . I'm sorry."

"But, yeah, I got with her the other night."

"You trust her?"

"I don't know, but I'm just going to lay low and see if what she's saying is legitimate. Says he's getting fifty bricks a week from Texas."

"Damn. The nigga is large."

"Yeah," Seven said seriously. "I just want to make sure my son is taken care of. You know, if anything happens to me, I want you to promise me you're going to take care of my little man."

"I got you. Don't even worry about it."

Seven continued, "Because it's going down. I'm talking about fifty bricks and a half a million dollars, you know."

"Yeah . . . life-changing money."

"Exactly."

"So the work come in on Wednesday," Butter repeated, almost to himself.

"Yeah."

"So, wha's the plan?"

"The plan is just to watch the shit unfold a couple of times, then we lick 'em. You know what I'm saying?"

"Yeah."

■

Two days later, Seven knocked on Adrian's door. When she opened he presented Adrian with four thousand dollars in cash. "I don't know how much the braces cost nor do I care. All I know is that I want my son to walk . . . Do you understand?"

"Yeah."

"The braces will make him walk, right?"

"The braces will *help* him walk; only he will make him walk."

"What the hell is that supposed to mean?"

"It means he still will have to have the willpower."

"He's just scared, that's all," Seven said. Then he stared at the ceiling for a moment, deep in thought. "I mean, just imagine trying something over and over and getting the same results. I just gotta get his confidence up, that's all."

"I think you're right."

"I got my mind made up and I gotta do."

Adrian looked at Seven, confused. "What is that supposed to mean?"

"Nothing . . . nothing, don't worry about it. I just want you to go to the doctor and pay for the braces, and whatever you have left . . . if you have anything left, put it aside for the operation . . . My boy *will* be walking," Seven said.

Adrian hugged Seven tight and he flexed his muscles. He remembered she liked that. They kissed and she whispered, "Please be careful."

"Don't worry about me . . . Nothing is going to happen to me."

CHAPTER 9

Wednesday morning in a subdivision in the northeastern part of town, a large black man was driving an F-150 with Texas license plates. He wore a large cowboy hat and boots. He was carrying a duffel bag.

Butter and Seven sat across the street, in Butter's Impala, watching the big man.

"Okay. He must be the connect," Seven said.

"Yeah. It looks like it."

"The nigga is huge."

"Yeah. That the type motherfucker you're going to have to give a bullet to," Butter said.

Seven pulled out his chrome nine millimeter. "And that's exactly what I intend to do."

"I know that's right. A bullet will stop that motherfucker."

"And I got them hollow points. You know?"

"I know, cuz. I got them too." Butter laughed.

"Yeah, this shit is going to be easy."

"It looks that way, but my only concern is those goons that Reno has with him."

"I thought about that too, but we don't have to worry about that. Supposedly, the connect doesn't like nobody to be around. I guess the nigga must be nervous with that kind of money," Seven said.

"I would too. That's a lot of money and product."

"Yeah. Elise is in there, though."

"Why the fuck would he let her be there when she's proving to be a snake?"

"I don't know, man. Some men are just weak for bitches."

"So, does she know when you're going to strike?"

"Hell no—you think I'm crazy? I'm not letting her know shit."

"Okay, good. I think we can lick them good."

"Yeah. This is going to be like taking candy from a baby."

"Yeah. I just want to watch this go down one more time."

"So, you're saying in two weeks."

"Exactly."

"What about now? We got to get money now, nigga. Bills is due."

"We'll just have to see somebody else for the time being."

"Okay. Maybe Black Kenny or Caesar."

"Shit; let's hit them both."

■

"Daddy, look at my leg braces," Tracey said.

"Yeah, my man is going to be able to walk now."

Tracey smiled and Seven stood him up.

Adrian smiled but said, "Not so fast, Seven, the braces are to help strengthen his legs . . . He still has to learn to walk."

"That's what I'm doing. I'm going to show him how to walk."

Seven held both of Tracey's arms and began to walk with him. Tracey took slow steps and laughed as his daddy held him. Once Seven let him go he looked confused and fell to the floor and started crying.

Seven picked him up. "It's going to be okay, son, you're doing good."

"I'm doing good," Tracey said, smiling.

"Yeah, he still needs therapy," Adrian said.

"Yeah, I know, but this is a good start. So how much was the braces?"

"About a thousand dollars."

"That's it?" Seven huffed. "You mean to tell me the whole time we've been running around here worrying about some damn braces that only cost a thousand dollars?"

"Well, I didn't know," she said.

"Didn't they tell you the cost of the braces?"

She sat on the sofa. "Well, they gave me the cost of the braces and the surgery, because to be honest the doctor thought the braces would help but he said eventually we would need the surgery."

"The surgery is what is going to cost. How much is it?" Seven asked.

"About twenty thousand dollars," Adrian replied.

"I'll have it in no time."

"Seven, I don't know about taking twenty thousand dollars into a doctor's office or a bank . . . you know they will question the shit out of me."

"What kind of questions?"

She huffed. Her facial expression said she couldn't believe he was asking such questions. "Duh . . . like where did the money come from? Like where do you work? Like your Social Security number to report the cash transaction to the Feds."

"I don't give a fuck about the Feds . . . Hell, do you need me to take them the money?"

"No, Seven, please, it will only be worse if you do it. A black man with that kind of cash? Please, you'll be back in jail in a heartbeat."

"So what do we do?"

"I'll give the money to my brother, he's been working for the prison system in Virginia for twenty-five years . . . He has hundreds of thousands of dollars in his pension. He can write the check and we won't have to worry about it."

"Cool." Seven smiled. He was happy because he really didn't want to take twenty thousand dollars into the doctor's office or the bank but if that was the only way he'd have to chance it. He walked over, grabbed Tracey by the arms, and walked with him. "You can do it, son, you can do it."

Tracey smiled as he continued to move his little feet.

■

Seven rang Caesar's doorbell. He was without a mask because he knew that Caesar didn't know him.

"Yeah, what do you want?" Caesar yelled.

"Do you own this blue Mercedes?"

"Yeah."

"I'm sorry, sir, but I accidentally backed into it."

When Caesar opened the door, Butter appeared with a blue bandana covering his face. "Okay, take us to the dope, nigga, or get a hole in your head."

"What are you talking about?" Caesar said.

Butter pushed Caesar back inside the house before anyone could see them.

"Now, let's get down to business. You know what we're here for."

"I don't have anything."

"Okay, but I do . . . like this .357, nigga, and I'm just dying to test it out—dying to see if they make holes as big as motherfuckers say they do."

Caesar held his hands up. "What do you want?"

Butter put the gun to his temple. "Don't talk unless I say you can talk. Is that understood?"

"Y-Yeah."

"Okay. Is there anybody in here with you?"

"No."

"Where's your wife and kid?"

"My mother-in-law's house."

"Where's the money?"

"Money? What money?" Caesar was still trying to play dumb.

"The money you better come up with or else you're going to die," Seven said.

"I got fifteen hundred dollars, man. That's all I got."

"Give us the money then, damn it," Butter ordered.

Caesar dug into his pocket and pulled out seven hundred-dollar bills. "The rest is in the bedroom, in a shoe box."

Seven led him to the bedroom. Caesar was about to grab a Nike shoe box when Seven said, "Let me get that." When he opened it, there was a chrome nine millimeter inside already cocked. Seven looked at Caesar angrily. "What the fuck were you planning to do with this?"

"N-Nothing man. Really."

Seven punched Caesar in his mouth.

"Give me the money," Butter demanded.

"I ain't got shit, man, really," Caesar said.

"Okay. You must be ready to die."

"No. Please don't kill me. Please don't hurt me. I promise I can get you some dope in the morning."

"Motherfucker, you won't be around in the morning unless you give me that money, man."

Caesar was sweating profusely. He said, "Hey, I have a ring that's worth twenty thousand dollars. It's a really nice ring in a platinum setting."

"Where is it?"

"It's in a jewelry box in the bathroom."

Seven kept the gun aimed at Caesar's head while Butter went to the bathroom. He returned with a little red jewelry box, which he opened.

"There's a million rings in here," Butter said.

"Hand me the box," Caesar said.

Butter passed Caesar the box. Caesar looked for a few moments until he found a woman's ring with a huge diamond.

"Damn, that motherfucker is beautiful," Seven said.

Caesar smiled. "Yeah, I think it's about six carats. I'm not sure but it's at least four."

Seven slapped Caesar with the gun and fired. "Oh, God. I'm dead!" Caesar screamed.

Butter and Seven laughed. Butter put a pillowcase over

Caesar's head. "Count to one hundred. If you take the pillowcase off your head, I'm killing you, nigga."

As Caesar began counting, Butter and Seven ran out the house, leaving the front door wide open.

■

"The lick has to go down smoothly, man," Seven said to Butter.

Butter was counting the money they had gotten for the ring. They had sold it to some old guy in north Charlotte for eight grand. He folded two stacks of hundred-dollar bills and placed them in his pocket. "I know, man."

"After we pull this one, we will be set."

"Well, we're going to have to be set, because everybody in the city is out to kill us, you know," Butter said.

"I don't give a fuck, man. I have to do this for my little boy, man. My son has to walk and be normal."

"I feel ya," Butter said. Then he folded another stack of bills and stuck them in his pocket. "I can't believe your man Caesar was so fucking easy."

"Yeah, I know. I couldn't believe that one either." Seven started laughing. "That coward was crying like a little girl."

"I know."

"I need something to smoke, man. Let's go get some weed. I wanna calm my nerves."

Seven and Butter hopped into the Impala and went to the corner store. Butter was headed inside when he noticed a light-skinned man on the side of the building dumping buds inside a cigar. He walked toward him. "Hey, man. I see you got that smoke."

The man smiled. "Yeah, this is the best shit . . . it's from my cousin from Cali."

"Oh, yeah? I got some smoke too, from Atlanta," Butter said.

"This is the best shit right here, my nigga, and nothing like that ATL bud."

"Hey, I'm going to go inside to get a couple of blunts and I'll be right back. I'll show you what we have. By the way, my name is Butter."

"Yella."

Butter stepped inside and grabbed a can of Bud Light and a pack of Swishers. When he returned, the man was smoking his blunt. He offered it to Butter.

"Naw; that's okay, but walk to the car with me. I'll show you what I got."

Butter and Yella reached the car. Seven was startled when he saw the stranger.

"Yo. This is my man, Yella. I was going to show him the bud we got," Butter said.

Seven opened the glove compartment and pulled out the sack of weed.

Yella laughed. “Oh, my shit is much better than that—much greener and everything.”

“Oh yeah?”

Yella dug into his pocket and pulled out the bag of buds and passed it to Butter.

“Yeah. This shit is fire.”

Seven asked, “Can you get more of this?”

“How much you need?”

“Maybe a pound or two.”

“I can get it. Just give me your number.”

Butter told him and Yella saved it to his cell phone.

■

When Butter and Seven pulled off they laughed.

“We got us another victim.”

“Yeah, we do. This is going to be easy. That motherfucker looks soft.”

“I’m going to hit him up later and tell him we need five pounds,” Butter said.

“Make it ten. I mean, if we’re going to make an enemy, we may as well go all out . . . don’t you think?”

“I feel ya.”

CHAPTER 10

Seven and Elise met at a Ramada Inn on the south end of the city. The clerk handed them the key and they got on the elevator to room 338.

"I can't believe you wanted to meet here," Seven said.

Elise looked confused. "Why not?"

"I thought, since you fucking with a drug lord and all, you'd want to stay at the W or the Marriott or some other fancy-assed hotel."

"Oh, whatever, boy."

When they entered their room, she said, "I'm tired of his ass."

"What's wrong?" Seven asked.

"I'm just at a point where I'm tired of looking at him. You know?"

"Just leave."

She fell silent.

"Elise, why don't you just leave?"

"I want to leave, but I don't know how. I mean, if I leave, I'm afraid that he will kill me."

"Well, that motherfucker has already threatened to kill me. Do you think I'm worried?"

"I know, but you're a man."

Seven looked in her eyes and saw that she really was afraid. "Hey. Don't worry about anything. Nothing is going to happen to you."

She sat on the bed and turned on CNN news. They were talking about the execution of Tookie Williams.

"That's sad," Elise said.

"What sad about it? I mean—it's life," Seven said.

"I mean, they're going to kill that man and he's turned his life around and made a difference."

"You know, you're really naïve. It doesn't really matter what you do once they put a label on you, like drug dealer, gangster, playa . . . that's it. Doesn't matter how many books you write, how many records you sell, you're still considered scum."

"But he's going to die."

"I know. Our heroes die. They all die: Martin, Malcolm, Tupac, and now Tookie. It's not sad; it's reality. Some must die in order for others to live."

She looked at him and finally said, "Seven, you're really smart."

"I've been told that before."

"Why do you act the way you do?"

He was confused. "I have no choice. I was wired to act like this. You were wired to act like this. We're a product of our experiences."

A tear trickled down her cheek. "I want us to be together."

"We will. Just wait until I get what I need from ya boy."

"When is that going to happen? I told you that he gets the package in on Wednesday."

"I know. You have to be patient. *We* have to be patient."

"And what are you doing in the meantime?"

He took a deep breath. He thought about Caesar and Black Kenny. "I'm just surviving, you know, the best way I can."

She pulled out ten hundred-dollar bills from her purse and handed it to him.

He folded the money and handed it back to her. "I can't take your money."

"Why not? I've got plenty."

"I bet you do, but it's just something about taking money from a woman I can't get with."

"Don't give me that bullshit, Seven. You're a fucking pimp nigga. That's what you do, use women."

He laughed. "But you can tell me where the stash is."

"The stash?"

"You know—where he keeps the money. The safe."

"Now, that I don't know."

"Come on. I know you know this."

She looked at him briefly before turning her head. "I've told you when he gets his product."

"I know, and it's going down, but I was just wondering when I get him should I get him to take me to the stash."

"I think you should just be content."

He thought hard. He envisioned himself inside the house, Reno lying facedown on the floor, crying like a bitch.

"Seven, I can tell you right now, you better plan this shit out or somebody could get seriously hurt," Elise said, interrupting his fantasy.

"Like I just said—sometimes people have to die in order for others to live. I ain't afraid to die. I ain't got shit to lose." He took off his shirt, revealing tattoos.

She grabbed him around the waist. Neither wanted the feeling to end.

■

Seven was about to step into his apartment when his phone rang. The caller ID said "Baby Mama."

"Yo."

"Hey, I need some money for day care," Adrian said.

"How much you need?"

"Like a hundred twenty dollars."

"Okay, I'll bring it in the morning. Is that okay?"

"Yeah, that's fine."

"How's Tracey doing?"

"He's asleep."

"Yeah? Give him a kiss for me. Will you?"

"Okay."

An awkward silence followed. Finally, Adrian said, "Seven, Tracey is getting heavy."

"What do you mean?"

"I mean, I'm a woman. I don't know if I can continue to pick him up. We have to do something."

"Maybe a stroller, or some kind of cart."

"No, Seven, I want my baby to walk, damn it! I want him to be normal, just like the rest of the kids."

Seven took a deep breath. "I want him to walk too. You think I enjoy not being able to see my son run around and play?"

"So what are we going to do about it?"

"I got a plan. Just hang in there with me."

"Seven, I hope your dumb ass ain't thinking about doing no illegal shit."

"No. I'm going to get a job, make a hundred thousand dollars a month and pay for my son's braces, his operation and his physical therapy."

"Oh, so you're being funny now."

"No. I'm getting pressure from my baby's mama."

"I don't mean to pressure you. I don't want you to go to jail."

"But what are we going to do if I don't get the money the way I know how?"

"There's the church . . . there's programs."

"Let me tell you something. I am a black man; a felon at that. I'm going to get the money the best way I know how."

"You're selling drugs again?"

"No."

"What are you doing, then? How are you going to get the money?" Adrian demanded.

Seven took a deep breath. "Don't worry about the money. Just know that I'm going to get it. I have to get it for my son's sake."

"I just want my son to have his father around."

"And he will." Again there was an awkward silence. Seven finally said, "I'll get you the money for the day care. I have to go now."

■

Butter knocked on Seven's door. It was almost 11 A.M. Seven was surprised to see him.

"What you doing here so early?"

"Nigga, it's almost noon. Let's get up and out. We have work to do."

"What kind of work?"

"Listen. You remember the cat we met at the store the other day?"

"Yeah?"

"I just hit him up and told him I needed three pounds of weed."

Seven took a seat on his sofa and turned the television on to Dr. Phil. "What did he say?"

"He said he had it."

"Oh yeah? Well, let's just call him back and tell him we need ten pounds."

Butter pulled out his cell phone. After three rings the man on the other end picked up.

"Hey, what up," Butter said.

"We still on?" Yella said.

"Yeah. I was just calling to find out if I could change my order to ten pounds."

Yella hung up. Seconds later Butter's phone rang. The caller ID said "Unknown Number." Butter almost didn't answer it. "Hello?"

"Yeah, this is Yella."

"Yeah. What happened?"

"Nothing happened. You just have to watch what ya say on my phone, man."

"Oh. I understand."

"Okay, I got what ya need. Where can you meet me?"

"Freedom Mall parking lot."

"The back side is cool," Yella said.

"Okay. I'll see ya in about twenty minutes."

■

Yella was driving a champagne-colored Cadillac when he pulled into the mall's parking lot. Butter spotted him when he rolled up. He hopped out of his car and got into the Caddy with Yella. "Okay, what ya got for me?"

Yella pulled out a small sack of weed and passed it to him.

"Where's the rest of it?

Yella looked surprised. "Where's your money?"

"I need to see the rest of the weed before I show you the money."

Someone tapped on Butter's window. When he looked up he saw a man standing there pointing a chrome handgun. "Motherfucker, what you need to do is give your fucking money or I'ma blow your brains out."

Seven saw everything. He grabbed his nine millimeter from under the seat and and stepped out of the car. He cocked his gun and aimed at the gunman.

"Nigga, don't even try it," a voice said from behind him. Seconds later Seven felt cold steel on the side of his neck.

He'd been at the mercy of a gun before. "Drop your fucking gun or else I'ma lodge one in your neck, nigga."

Seven's mind raced as he thought about how he and Butter had been robbed in New York; about all the promises he'd made while he was in the pen about not turning back to a life of crime; but more important he thought about Tracey. His little boy needed him. "Hey, man, I got two pounds of chronic in the car," Seven lied, trying to buy time, trying to read the man with the gun.

"You do?"

"Yeah, I'll get it for you." Seven knew if he could make it back inside the car, he could get to the piece Butter had hidden there. He took two steps toward the car.

"Hold the fuck up, I'm giving the goddamned orders, don't you move unless I say move . . . understand?" the man said as he turned out Seven's pockets. He opened his wallet. "A hundred forty-three dollars, nigga? Where's the rest of it?"

"I don't have no money, man, honestly I don't."

"So what the fuck y'all niggas came here for, was y'all coming to rob?"

"No, man, we just wanted to see the product," Seven found himself saying. He felt like such a coward.

The first man ordered Butter, "Get out, bitch, and lay facedown. As a matter of fact you walk over there beside your friend."

Butter did what he was told. As he headed toward Seven, he spotted a white SUV with the word SECURITY etched on the door. Suddenly Butter waved his hands wildly and yelled "Help!"

The SUV sped over toward the scene. An old white man rolled down his window slowly. "What's going on?"

One of the gunmen said, "Mind your goddamned business, old man—or else."

The security guard slammed the car into reverse when he saw the guns—but not before calling for backup on his radio.

The gunman said, "Oh you're a old wannabe-hero-ass old-man." He blasted the SUV's tires. Seconds later, another SUV appeared. The gunmen jumped into the Cadillac and fled the scene.

■

Inside the mall interrogation room, a young white rookie cop with freckles and red hair named Donahue scribbled on a yellow legal pad.

"Who were the men?"

"I don't know," Seven said.

"Come on, man, I know you know something," an older black detective said.

"I'm telling you they came out of nowhere, never seen them before in my life."

"Okay, out of all the people in the mall they rob you and your friend."

"I guess so."

The rookie cop looked at the detective, then said, "Your partner said they thought you had drugs."

Seven knew the games the cops played. He knew they lied; he'd been interrogated many times and he knew what to say and what not to say. He would never cooperate with them—it was just against every moral fiber in his body.

"Remember, your friend is the one that flagged the security guard, so you know he done told us what we want to know," the detective said.

"Well, if he done told you what you want to know, why do you need my story?" Seven asked logically.

"You want to be a hard-ass, huh? Why don't you just admit they were robbing you for drugs?"

Seven looked at the cop with piercing eyes. "Am I under arrest?"

"No."

He stood and walked out of the interrogation room.

■

Butter was waiting in the car. When Seven opened the door, Butter smiled. “That was a close call.”

“Yeah, it damn sure was.”

“So what did you tell them?” Butter asked.

“I ain’t tell them shit.”

“Me either.”

“The white cop said you said they were try’na get us for drugs.”

Butter laughed. “Come on, man, you know we were trying to get *them* for drugs.”

“That’s why they sounded ridiculous trying to get me to say something.”

Butter lit up a blunt. “Man, ain’t that some shit! We were try’na rob them niggas and they robbed our ass.”

“Yeah, the fucked-up part about it is we could’ve gotten killed.”

“Nah, don’t think they would have killed us in public.”

“Yeah, but shit was real out there. I hadn’t never really thought about dying till then . . . you know, all kinds of shit go through your head, like your kids and your funeral.”

Butter was silent. They both had been vulnerable looking down the barrel of a gun. They both were human. Finally Butter uttered, “Death is so final.”

Seven mumbled, “I know.”

CHAPTER 11

Caesar was pumping gas into a White Tahoe when Butter spotted him.

"Hey, there's that faggot-assed nigga Caesar."

"Yeah, looks like the motherfucker ain't doing too bad," Seven said.

"Yeah, he got twenty-six-inch rims on his truck and everything."

Butter pulled the Impala in front of the Tahoe. He jumped out of the car and grabbed Caesar from behind. "Get in my car, playboy."

Caesar tried to run but he was met by Seven. "Nigga, I think you need to come with us."

Seven held his arm, walked him to the Impala and jumped in the backseat with him.

Caesar continued to struggle but Seven's grip was too firm. "Where are you taking me? What about my truck?"

"I don't give a fuck about your truck," Seven said.

"You know what we need," Butter added.

"I don't have no dope or money, man," Caesar cried.

"No, what you don't have is a life if you don't put us on," Seven said.

Butter drove down a dark road and parked the car. He turned and slapped Caesar as hard as he could. "Nigga, who is your connect?"

"Connect, what are you talking about?"

"Talking about throwing a dead body in the Catawba River if you don't tell me who your connect is."

Seven tightened his grip around Caesar's neck. Caesar turned red. "I can't breathe, man."

"Who is the connect, nigga," Butter demanded.

"I don't—" Caesar lost his breath.

Butter hopped out the car. "Get out of the car with him, Seven."

Seven opened the door with one hand. The other arm was still around Caesar's neck.

Butter got a baseball bat from the trunk and walked around to the passenger side. "Aight, motherfucker, get out the car!"

Seven relaxed his grip. Caesar bounced out of the car but before he could run Seven was gripping his neck again. "Don't try no dumb shit."

"Okay, who is the connect, Caesar?" Butter asked.

"I don't have a connect."

"Nigga, one more lie and I'm busting your fucking kneecaps!"

"Listen, man, I don't know what you're talking about," Caesar protested.

Butter swung the bat but Caesar moved and he hit Seven instead. "Ouch, motherfucker!" Seven said, but he still managed to hold Caesar in his grip.

Butter swung again. This time the bat hit Caesar's left kneecap.

"Oh God, please don't hit me again!" Caesar howled as he crumpled to the ground. Seven let him go; he wasn't going anywhere now.

Butter's face became serious. "This time, nigga, I'm cracking your cranium. Tell me where you getting the dope from."

Caesar made eye contact with Butter but didn't say anything.

"Motherfucker, I'm going to crack your legs and throw you in the river, nigga."

Seven began to choke Caesar again. "Nigga, you think we playing?"

"No," he managed to say. "Can you tell him to let me breathe?"

"Loosen up a bit, Seven."

Seven released his grip. "Okay. Who is the connect, nigga?"

"His name is JoJo . . . JoJo Ingram."

"So the nigga is holding, huh?"

"Yeah, he got bricks and shit. I heard the nigga had a connection in Miami, where he's getting X and blow, but I know he has a couple of million, you know."

"Million?"

"Yeah, but I doubt he has it in his home."

Seven looked at Caesar with intense eyes. He then thought if they could rob JoJo and then Reno, he would be set. He could pay for his son's operation and leave North Carolina.

"So where does he live?" Butter asked.

"The University area . . . you know, up there by the race-track."

"Damn, that fool live a long way from here." Butter held the tip of the bat to Caesar's head. "Nigga, this better not be no funny shit."

■

JoJo lived in a big two-story house across from a lake on a dark road. A Cadillac Escalade and a white Benz were in the driveway. "Okay, is the nigga at home?" Butter wanted to know.

"Yeah, he's there: His wife drives the Benz and he drives the Escalade," Caesar replied.

"He has an alarm," Seven said, noticing the sign.

"Yeah, but it's early, only seven P.M.," Butter said. "He probably hasn't even set the alarm yet."

Seven made eye contact with Caesar. "He has a wife, huh?"

"Yeah."

"Kids?"

"No kids . . . none that I know of."

Butter grinned. "This is going to be a piece of cake." He hit the accelerator and drove out of the subdivision down a long, winding, dark road. He parked the car and ordered Caesar to step out and get into the trunk.

Caesar looked confused. "Are you kidding, man?"

"No, get your punk ass in the trunk," Seven said.

Caesar did so reluctantly. Butter jumped on the highway and fifteen minutes later he was at his house. He retrieved masks and gloves, his .380 and a sawed-off shotgun. When he got in the car he handed Seven the shotgun with a pair of gloves and a mask. "My adrenaline is going, nigga."

"I feel ya," Seven said. "I hope the nigga has a stash—you know I need money more than anything."

■

Only the crickets chirped on the quiet street. Butter was in the front of the house and Seven was watching out for him on the side. The door hinges came off easily when Butter's size-13 shoe hit it. The good news was the alarm wasn't set. He and Seven ran up the stairs. When he got to the top of the stairs he saw a short dark man punching numbers in a cell phone, rushing to the rear of the house. "Drop the goddamn phone," Butter said.

The man dropped the phone. "What do you want?"

"We want the cash, nigga."

The man held his arms in plain view. "The money is in the room."

"Hey, what's going on?" a female voice said.

Startled, Butter turned and fired twice. The first bullet hit her chest and the next one tore through her abdomen. The woman crashed to the floor.

JoJo screamed. "Oh my God, Nia, please . . . why did you shoot my wife? I was going to give you the money, why did you have to shoot?"

Seven turned to Butter. "Yeah, why did you shoot?"

"She scared me, man."

JoJo rushed over to his wife, who lay there bleeding.

Butter aimed the gun at him. "You get back, motherfucker."

JoJo grabbed his wife's hand, ignoring Butter's order. "Hang in there, baby, please hang in there."

She looked up at him and tried to speak but couldn't.

JoJo began to cry. "Baby, it's going to be all right."

She said, "The baby . . ."

Seven said, "What is this crazy bitch talking about?"

JoJo looked up at Butter and then Seven. "My wife is pregnant."

"Oh no, damn, what have I gotten myself into?" Seven said.

Butter looked at Seven. "I'm sorry, man, really I am, but I didn't know if she was going to try to hurt me or not, so I had to do what I had to do."

"You fucked up, nigga," Seven said.

"Fuck all that mushy shit," Butter said. Then he grabbed JoJo by the arm. "Take me to the room, give me the fucking money and we're out of here."

Inside the room the man opened a Nike shoe box that was filled with hundred-dollar bills. "Here's ten thousand."

"I know you got more than that," Butter said.

"No, I really don't."

Butter aimed the gun at the man. "You really want this to be a fucking massacre in here?"

Seven shouted, "Come on, nigga, we gotta get out here, this woman is going to die!"

He dashed down the stairs and Butter followed.

When they got inside the car, Seven said, "We have to get rid of Caesar."

"I know."

"But what are we going to do with him?"

Butter fired up the ignition and drove out of the neighborhood, screeching his tires. "Don't worry, I got an idea."

■

Caesar stood on the bank of the Catawba River, a SpongeBob pillowcase on his head. His hands were bound with tape and he had leg irons on. Butter shot him two times in the head. SpongeBob turned from yellow to maroon. When Caesar fell to the ground, Butter and Seven picked him up and tied cinder blocks to his feet and tossed him in the river. Then they walked back to the car.

"Damn, I didn't want it to go that far," Seven said.

"Me either but you know he would have snitched, so we had no choice," Butter said.

"I know, but we got other shit to worry about, like that pregnant woman. I hope she made it," Seven said.

"Worst comes to worst, if we're caught the most I can get is attempted murder."

"I know but let's not think about that. Nothing is going to happen."

They got into the car and drove off. Neither man said anything. Seven let his window down. He needed cool air and he needed time to think. He'd have to go back to New York but he had no money. He had a son to think about and that son couldn't walk. He turned the music on. Tupac's song "Blasphemy" was playing. He tried to bop his head to the beat. He tried to get his mind off the situation but he couldn't. Finally, he turned the music down and called Elise. She didn't answer. He then called Adrian; she answered on the third ring. He could tell she'd been sleeping

"I want to come see my son."

"This time of night? Can't you wait till in the morning?"

"No, I want to see him now."

"Seven, have you been drinking?"

"No, I sure haven't."

"Okay, come on, but hurry."

He terminated the call. "I need you to take me to my baby's mom's house."

"I heard the conversation."

Seven looked at Butter angrily. "You know, you really done some stupid shit today, man."

Butter pulled the car to the side of the road. "Hey man, I don't want to hear that shit! What's done is done."

"Fuck, you didn't have to shoot the woman."

"I didn't know it was a woman, man! I didn't know."

"She was pregnant too, man, the bitch was pregnant."

"I know she was pregnant, I heard her lame-ass husband."

"No, nigga, you're the fucking lame-ass . . . you're the one shooting pregnant bitches."

Butter cocked the hammer of his gun and pointed it at Seven.

"Shoot me, motherfucker, shoot me—I don't give a fuck. My life is worthless anyway now thanks to you."

Butter lowered the gun and pressed the accelerator. Neither man said anything until they reached Adrian's house. Butter said, "Yo, Seven, man, I'm sorry, man, I really fucked up this time."

Seven gave him five. "Hey, we're going to be okay. We're in this together; don't worry."

■

Seven kissed Adrian on her cheek and headed straight to his son's room, woke him up and carried him to the sofa. Little Tracey lay on Seven's chest; every so often he'd wake up, look at his dad and smile. Seven's mind raced. The night had been a long one and he'd been an accomplice to a murder. At least one; he still didn't know if the pregnant woman had died or not. He ran his fingers through his little boy's hair. He wished he could hold his son forever but deep inside he knew he couldn't.

CHAPTER 12

Adrian was looking at *Daybreak News* when Seven woke up. "Good morning," he said as he laid little Tracey on the sofa and got up to stretch.

"Good morning," she said.

"Up really early, aren't you?"

"Yeah, I like to catch the news, you know."

"See anything interesting?" he asked.

"Just the usual; drug bust here, a shooting there, a stabbing there."

"Yeah, I know; it's depressing, huh."

She went to the kitchen and poured a cup of coffee. "But there was a home invasion in East Charlotte . . . A pregnant woman got killed."

"Killed?"

"Yeah, they said two gunmen invaded her home and killed her. She was six months' pregnant."

"Did the baby die?" Seven asked.

"Yeah . . . that's sad," Adrian said, then sipped her coffee. "Whoever did that shit need to rot in hell."

Seven remained silent. Finally, he disappeared into the bathroom and called Butter. The call went straight to voice mail. Seven walked back into the living room area. The news was still on.

"Hey, can I turn it to ESPN?"

"Shh." Adrian turned the television up. "Listen to this."

Seven turned his attention to the television. Footage of the Petro Express. Caesar's truck appeared on the screen. Then his face. The newscaster said, "Caesar Palo was abducted from this gas station last night about eight P.M. Security cameras caught the incident." Butter's car was now on the screen and then the license plate was blown up.

Seven was nervous but luckily the pictures of him and Butter were unclear. Adrian couldn't possibly recognize him.

"Damn, people are crazy out here."

"Yeah, I know what ya mean," Seven said.

"That car kind of reminds me of your friend Butter's car," she said.

"Come on, you know everybody in the South got Impalas and shit, that car don't look nothing like his car."

"Yes, it does too."

"No it don't," he said angrily.

She looked at him, confused. "What the hell is all of that about?"

"Nothing . . . I'm sorry."

She looked at him and he avoided her eyes. "Seven, did you have something to do with abducting that man?"

"No."

"Come on, Seven, you can tell me. I'm not going to turn ya in."

His conscience ate away at him. "Listen, I did . . . I mean, we did . . . Butter and me."

She shook her head. "Seven, no you didn't."

"I didn't mean to do it."

"Do what?"

"Nothing."

"Seven, where is that man?"

"Nowhere."

"Come on, you have to tell me so I can help you."

He grabbed her hand. He thought about his history with her—how he met her while he was locked up. How she never told a soul that she was having sex with him when he was an inmate. He knew he could trust her. "The man is dead."

"What do you mean, he's dead?"

"He's dead. We had to kill him."

She paced; tears began to stream down her face. "Oh this

is just fucking great! The father of my child is going *back* to prison."

"I'm not going anywhere."

"Seven, why did you kill that man?"

"I didn't kill him, Butter did."

"You were with him."

Seven looked away. He knew he'd really fucked up this time. If they were caught he'd be charged with possibly three murders in the *South*. He knew that those overzealous prosecutors loved to put away black men from New York City.

"Why did you kill him, Seven?"

"We didn't want to do it but we had to."

"Did you rob him?"

"No."

Tracey woke up and noticed his mama and daddy fussing. He started crying. Seven walked over to his son, picked him up and looked at Adrian. "You scared him."

■

"Nigga, they got us on the news," Seven said to Butter over the phone.

"What the fuck are you talking about?"

"I was watching the news this morning and the security camera at the Petro Express caught us on tape, nigga, they got your car, showed your license plate and everything."

"Damn," Butter said, then he fell silent. "We don't need to talk over the phone. I'm coming over."

"Make sure you don't come in your car."

■

When Seven opened the door Butter was visibly shaken. Seven led him to the kitchen and handed him a bottle of water. "What are we going to do?"

"We have get out of here," Seven replied.

"We don't have no damn money, man! How can we get out of here?"

Seven took a deep breath. "I don't know."

"I fucked up, man, I'm sorry; I really fucked up this time."

"What's done is done—we have to deal with it," Seven said.

Butter drank the whole bottle of water in almost one swallow. Seconds later Adrian walked into the kitchen. "What are *you* doing here?" she said to Butter.

He looked confused. "What are you talking about? What do you mean, what am *I* doing here?"

"Nigga, you killed that man."

Butter stood up from the table and glared at Seven.

"Nigga, you put this bitch in our business? What kind of shit is that?"

"She saw the fucking car on the news."

Butter threw his hands up. "Oh, that's all I need now is a ho in my business."

"Nigga, your faggot ass is in big fucking trouble. Do you know you're about to be charged with a triple murder?"

Butter and Seven both said, "What are you talking about?"

"Talking about Butter's car being spotted in the neighborhood where the pregnant woman was murdered. Talking about an old white man calling the car in."

"Shit."

"Yeah, motherfucker, you don't have to worry about me; it's these Good Samaritan–ass white folks that gonna do ya dumb ass in," Adrian said.

Butter walked toward the living room but Seven stopped him.

"Where are you going, man?"

"I don't know."

"Listen, we have to stick together—we can't just split up now."

Butter's face became serious. "What are you talking about? I think the best thing for us to do is go our separate ways, man."

"No, we have to get outta here but we gotta do it together, man."

"Everything we've ever done together has gone sour, nigga. It's time for us to split up."

"Hey, man, we need money and you know what' s going down on Wednesday?"

"What're you talking about?"

"Reno's shipment comes in." Seven smiled. "We gotta get him, man. If we get him we'll have enough money to run with."

Butter didn't say anything for a while. Finally he nodded. "You're right."

CHAPTER 13

even convinced Adrian to rent a Lincoln Navigator so he and Butter could roll on the DL. Right now they were following the black man in the white F-150 with Texas license plates. When he turned, Seven would turn. When he slowed up, so did they, always managing to stay at least two car lengths away, until they were about two miles from Reno's stash house. Seven had hoped the man would pull over to get some gas or something. This would have enabled them to put the gun to his chest and order him to drive them to the stash house.

Seven's mind raced. Who was this dude? Was he packing a gun? If so, what kind? Seven pulled his gun out and took it off safety. They need him to stop, but how? He got an idea.

When they were about a mile away from Reno's stash house he slammed into the back of the truck.

The driver stopped and jumped out of the car in a flash.

He was a big man, in jeans and cowboy boots. "Damn, this motherfucker done ruined my truck."

Seven jumped out of the Navigator. "Hey, man, I'm sorry." He extended his hand to the man.

The man refused the handshake. "Why didn't just watch where you were going?"

"Listen, man, I have insurance, everything is going to be okay."

"Don't even worry about it. I'm in a hurry, man, I'm going to let this one slide. You don't owe me shit," the man said as he walked back to the truck.

Butter got out the car with a Desert Eagle. "But, motherfucker, you owe us."

"Oh shit," the man said.

"Oh shit is right, nigga," Butter said. "Get back in your truck—I'm riding with you. If you make one motherfuckin' false move, I'ma tear your whole chest apart."

"Come on, man, go easy with the gun. What do you want, money? Dope?"

"Get in the car," Butter said.

"Who sent you? Reno?"

Butter put the gun in the man's back. "Quit asking all these damn questions."

Big Texas got in the truck and Butter got in on the passenger side and Seven followed close behind in the Navigator. When they were in Reno's driveway, Butter said, "Where is the dope?"

"On the bed of the truck," Big Texas replied.

Seven took the cover off the truck and got the two duffel bags and loaded them into the Navigator.

Someone peered through the window of Reno's home. Seconds later Big Texas's phone rang. "Who in the hell is that with you?" The voice was loud enough for Butter and Seven to hear clearly.

"We're your cousins—you need us to help you carry the product," Butter said in a low tone.

"My cousins, man; I needed them to carry the product," Big Texas repeated into his cell.

"Aight, hurry, 'cause I have somewhere to be."

■

When Reno opened the door Butter placed the barrel of the Desert Eagle to his face and smiled. "Didn't think you would see us again, huh?"

Seven had the .380 pointed at Tex.

"What the fuck are you doing?" Reno glanced at Tex. "Nigga, you set me up?"

"No, they followed me, man."

Butter grabbed Reno's arm. "Nigga, ain't no time to discuss what went wrong. I need the money."

"Lay facedown, big guy," Seven ordered Big Tex. The big man complied.

Elise walked out of the bedroom and Reno made eye contact with her. "All the shit I done for you and you repay me like this."

"I don't know what you're talking about," Elise said.

"Your motherfuckin' 'brother' is what the fuck I'm talking about."

"Where is the goddamned money, nigga! One more word out of your ass and I swear you ain't gonna have no head," Butter said. "Do you know what kind of damage this gun can do?"

"The money is in the den," Reno said.

Seven turned his head to the side and cocked his gun. "Okay, bitch-assed nigga, take me to the den."

Reno and Elise walked ahead of Seven.

Elise was trembling. She'd recognized that look in Seven's eyes. It was the same look he had when he'd assaulted her.

Reno motioned to the wall safe.

"Don't just stand there pointing to the safe, I need that money now. Open the goddamned safe!" Butter was almost ready to lose it.

Reno did. The money was in thick bundles, at least a hundred bundles. Seven smiled. "How much money?"

"About five hundred thousand," Reno said.

Seven moved toward the safe. "Butter," he yelled, "come back here and help me."

Seconds later Butter walked in with Big Tex in front of him with his hands on his head.

"Face the wall," Butter said.

"Get over there with your friend," Seven told Tex.

Both men faced the wall across from the safe.

"Elise, get me something to put this money in," Seven ordered.

Elise disappeared and came back with two large pillowcases. She handed them to Seven.

Butter kissed the money as he loaded the cases.

"Boy, this is our lucky day, nigga, we got money *and* dope," Seven said. Then he quickly remembered that he was probably wanted for Caesar's death and the death of the pregnant woman. He suddenly felt nauseous.

Butter walked over to Tex and Reno and yelled, "I need y'all to be butt motherfuckin' naked."

"What kind of shit is this?" Reno said.

Butter looked Reno in his eyes. "I need you to do what I say, Mr. Big Man, or else."

Both men pulled their pants to their knees.

"Close your eyes and hold hands," Butter said.

Seven looked at Elise. He knew she was weak; she'd betrayed him before. She knew too much about him and how he operated. She'd probably squeal. He couldn't chance it. "Get over there in the center of the two men," he ordered.

She looked terrified. "What's going on, Seven . . . why?"

"Just do it."

Elise held the two naked men's hands. Seven walked out the door. Seconds later Butter let off three shots. The three corpses lay still holding hands.

When Butter stepped out the door he held onto a bag of money and met Seven pointing a nine millimeter.

"Drop your gun, B."

Butter looked confused. "Quit playing, nigga."

Seven's face was serious. "I ain't playing, nigga."

Butter laughed and said, "Quit playing," again.

Seven fired the nine millimeter three times. Two shots hit Butter in his chest and the third hit him in the neck. He gagged on his own blood.

Seven smiled. "Sorry, homey."

"Fuck you" were Butter's last words.

Seven took the bag of money from Butter. He crossed his heart and looked to the sky. "Forgive me, Lord." *Niggas will kill over life-changing money,* he thought.

■

Adrian opened the door of the apartment for Seven at 2 A.M. She noticed the worried look on his face. "What's wrong, baby?"

"Nothing."

She frowned. "Seven, I know you."

Seven thought about all the people that were dead and he knew he couldn't tell her that he'd killed Butter. He changed the subject. "Where is my boy?"

"He's asleep."

"Why is it so damn hot in here?"

"The air conditioner broke."

Beads of sweat rolled down his face into his eye. "I want to get me some rest, cuz in the morning I'm out of here, I gotta go."

Seven opened one of the pillowcases and showed her some money—about two hundred thousand dollars.

"What the fuck . . . How did you get this money?" Adrian demanded.

"Don't worry about it. Just use it wisely. I'll be in touch . . . make sure my boy gets the best surgeon money can buy." He kissed her on her forehead. "Nothing is going to happen to me."

"Where's Buttter? What's he going to do?"

"I don't know what he's going to do; that's not my concern. All I know is what I'm going to do and that's take care of my family."

"How the hell are you going to take care of us on the run? Don't you know there will be a manhunt out for you soon?"

"I know, but I don't give a fuck."

She looked stern. "You took lives."

"I did it for a just cause."

"The police will kill you if they catch you."

"I don't care. I did it for y'all—you and Tracey," Seven said as he began to pace.

"Don't justify it, Seven," she said with tears streaming down her face.

"Please don't start that crying bullshit! Everything is going to be okay, I promise everything is going to be all right," Seven said. His heart was beating fast. He knew things would never be okay again but it just seemed like the right thing to say. "I'm not justifying anything. I'm just saying I had to do what I had to do."

She looked at him but didn't say anything. "I love you, Seven, I've always loved you."

"I know." He avoided her eyes.

"I've got family in Arizona, I want you to go there."

"Okay, I'll go in the morning."

He walked into the bedroom. His son was lying on the bed with his bow legs sprawled. The window was up to cool the room. Seven kissed him and picked him up and laid him on his chest. Little Tracey smiled when he saw his dad. Seven was afraid. He knew that if he was caught he would get at least life—probably the death penalty—for the crimes he'd commited. Hell, seven people were dead! He'd honestly thought he would make it in the South. He'd seen many players from his New York neighborhood fall prey to the system. Some had gotten life for drugs; others had gotten gunned down in the streets; others were on drugs. He was surprised he'd lived to be twenty-eight.

Tracey said, "I love you, Daddy."

Seven kissed him again. Adrian got in the bed beside them. Seven hugged and kissed both of them throughout the night trying not to think about his situation.

The next morning when Adrian awoke, Seven was gone.

■

Seven drove the Navigator into South Carolina, down a dark, dusty road. He put some of his personal belongings in the truck: some pants, a shirt, a Yankees cap and a pair of sunglasses, plus a Louis Vuitton wallet with his ID. His and Butter's ski masks lay on the floor of the truck.

He hopped out of the truck and doused it with gasoline.

Then he stepped back and tossed a lighter. The Navigator went up in flames quickly.

He was glad this was all behind him. He didn't know what the future would hold for him, whether he would wind up in jail or remain on the run for the rest of his life, but he was glad this lifestyle was behind him—the ski mask way.

Seven cried quietly for Butter. They'd had a lot of good times together, but Butter had been stupid, he told himself, trying to justify the killing. But Seven knew the real reason he killed Butter—the greed had consumed him. The lick had been worth $500,000 and he hadn't wanted to share it with Butter. Now the money was all his, but where would he go? What would he do? He hadn't planned his escape but he knew he had to get the hell out of town and fast.

■

Catawba Lot was about a mile from the fire. It was a pretty big trailer park. Seven dashed between two trailers to a blue Honda Accord. The passenger door was unlocked. He broke the ignition, used a screwdriver to crank the car and drove away. He drove to D.C. and caught the Amtrak to Penn Station. He'd never been so glad to see New York City in his life but he knew he couldn't stay for long. He would have to keep it moving. He would move to Seattle or Portland, Oregon . . . he had to keep moving . . .

■

Seven watched the tall kid with the wavy hair on the soccer field in South Charlotte—number 7—running, jumping, kicking just like the rest of the kids. His legs were straight and he was handsome. Seven smiled. He wanted to say something to his son but he couldn't: He was dead; at least, that was what everybody thought and he couldn't just contact Tracey and Adrian just yet, he didn't want to alarm them.

Tracey kicked the ball hard into the goal and Seven cheered. But he was so far away nobody could really see him.

Did he have any regrets for helping his son? No. Did he regret killing Butter and Elise? Yeah, kind of, but he could have gotten killed or wound up in prison for the rest of his life. Sometimes people have to die in order for others to live.

TURN THE PAGE FOR EXCERPTS
OF MORE G-UNIT BOOKS
from 50 Cent

DEATH BEFORE DISHONOR

By 50 Cent

and

Nikki Turner

HIGH SPEED CHASE

As Trill cruised through the little hick town of Ashland, he consciously abided by all the laws. It didn't matter, though, because the sheriff was sure he had hit the lotto when he spotted his mark: a young black male driving a $60,000 truck. The Hummer happened to be Sheriff Bowman Body's dream truck. A truck he could only dream of having with his salary, and he despised the fact that some punk who probably never even finished high school was riding around in it.

Trill could have been wearing a priest's collar, but as far as Bowman Body was concerned, he was a drug dealer and a prime victim of the monthly driving citation quota. Before Trill could think twice, the sheriff's blue lights were bouncing off of his rearview mirror.

"Fuck!" Trill shouted. He beat his hand on the steering wheel as he spat the word out. He quickly looked down and, after making sure that his secret hiding place was secure, then pulled over. He watched from his side mirror as the small, thin-featured sheriff approached the car. His walk was like Forrest Gump but his look was the Terminator, coming to devour.

"License and registration, boy!" the sheriff said with authority as he knocked on the driver's side window.

Trill rolled down the window halfway. "No problem, officer," he responded, and leaned forward to the glove box to retrieve his registration.

"Freeze!" The sheriff drew his gun and sticking his hand inside the car.

Stunned, Trill slowly eased back into the driver's seat until he felt the tip of the sheriff's revolver at his temple.

"I was going for my registration, man," Trill said slowly. "Don't most people keep their registration in the glove box?"

"You trying to get fresh with me, nigger?" The sheriff cocked his gun.

Trill could feel his blood boiling. Given the opportunity, he would leave the racist redneck stinkin' on the hood of his own police cruiser for his fellow officers to scrape him off.

"You would think that you niggers would know the drill

by now, and have these things prepared," the sheriff drawled boldly. "As much shit as y'all stay in, you'd think y'all would pin the damn registration to your collars. Now slowly," Bowman Body said, ''open the glove box and retrieve the registration." He paused before adding, "And I said slowly, not like you grabbing for the last piece of chicken out of a bucket of Colonel Sanders."

Trill smelled the scent of trouble like shit from a three-hundred-pound man who just got an enema. He knew Barney Fife was gon' fuck with him until he came up with a reason good enough to stick him. Trill was fully aware that the four thousand grams of crack cocaine in his hiding spot was 3,400 grams more than enough to get him a mandatory life sentence in a federal penitentiary. His intincts told him that he didn't want to trust his life on the chance that this hillbilly didn't impound the truck and stumble up on the stash box. He had to make a move. His next move would be crucial. Trill knew he had 3.400 grams of a reason to give Bowman Body a run for his money. And he intended to do just that.

Trill grabbed the registration from the glove box and turned to hand it to the sheriff. When the sheriff reached inside the truck with his free hand and grabbed hold of the registration, Trill quickly hit the switch to roll the window up while he floored the accelerator at the same time. The powerful Hummer snatched the sheriff off his feet so fast he dropped the pistol, screaming while Trill put the pedal to the metal.

"Who the fuck reaching now? Get yo' hand out the chicken box, cracker!" Trill screamed at Bowman Body. "Get yo shit out my chicken box, motherfucker!" His adrenaline was pumping, having the upper hand. He knew if he was caught he was gone for life. So he was going out like a real-live gangsta—with a mean fight.

He drove the Humdinger like he was on safari in Africa; the sheriff hung from the side of the car, holding on for dear life, slamming into the door every now and then as the truck dragged him at sixty miles an hour down the road. He went from Barney Fife to Barney Rubble as he ran alongside the automobile.

Bowman Body was swinging from side to side, praying and calling out every scripture in the Bible he'd ever known from his childhood days going to vacation Bible School. Once Trill felt like he was deep enough in the sticks and had room and leeway to run and hide, he pushed the window's button down to release the sheriff and slammed on the brakes, throwing the sheriff facefirst to the ground.

Trill knew that the truck was going to be hot and keeping the beautiful machine would not be an option. This was most likely the only deserted stretch of road he was going to find. He grabbed a piece just in case he had to go to war, pulled off the road and got out of the truck. When Trill opened up the door, Bowman Body was crawling on his belly like a frontline soldier. He was relentless and wasn't going to give up easily. He managed to lunge forward and grab Trill's leg to try to slow him down. Trill laughed at first. He couldn't believe the motherfucker was on his heels. But after he tried to wiggle his leg loose to no avail, he got pissed off.

Trill kicked the sheriff in his face with his new Timbs. Bowman Body's head hit a rock, causing him to bleed like Rick Flare in a cage match. Blood gushed out all over the pavement. Trill didn't waste time. Although his shoes had blood on them, he took off running like a jaguar in the wild. He was mad that he didn't have on the fresh Jordans that he copped earlier from the mall, but Timbs were good in any kind of weather. It was unlikely that the police would find the drugs, but if they did, it wouldn't matter. Trill's only concern at this point was to get away. He took comfort in knowing that the registered owner of the vehicle didn't know him from a can of paint. He'd paid a friend to pay a friend $10,000 to put the Hummer in their name. Maybe the best 10,000 he'd ever spent; it pays to think ahead.

It felt like hours as Trill trudged through the trees, mud, rocks and small streams of water. Out of breath and panting, he found a tree to rest against. He knew that he would be there until sundown. Some hunter stopped to help the sheriff, and of course by now backup was on the way, but at least Trill had gotten a fairly decent head start. But no sooner had Trill thought the fading sun was his answer than he heard a sound that put him on the run again. And he needed to move fast. Trill knew he had to shed some weight. As much as he hated to part with it, the first thing to go was his brand-new chinchilla jacket.

The sound of blood hounds let Trill know that backup and probably some deputized citizens with shotguns were on the scent of his trail. He wasn't too much worried about the bloodhounds; his main concern was them redneck hill-billies who could smell a nigga a mile away. The man hunt was on.

As the pursuit continued, Trill knew that they were closing in on him. Not only was the sound of the hounds getting closer, he could hear the hum of a helicopter entering the area. He couldn't see it yet, but the sound of the whirling blades were distinctive. And just because he couldn't see it didn't mean that it couldn't see him. He knew he was doomed. But he trudged through the woods anyway, hoping no one in the distant houses would see him and give him up. He had no idea where he was going or where he'd end up. The only destination he had in mind was to get the fuck out of redneck county!

■

As Sunni stood in her kitchen warming up some leftover hot wings from the day before, she went to wash off the sauce that had gotten on her hands. As she looked out of the window over the sink, she could have sworn that she saw something. It was dark, and the light was on in the kitchen, so she could barely see. She flipped the light switch off, allowing her a better view of the rear of her house, and there it was again. It was a person; a black man, and then she zeroed in on the helicopter overhead. When she looked back down from the helicopter, she found herself staring into the eyes of someone in her backyard. She jumped, and a scream slipped out, but then she felt a sense of familiarity. It was the same guy from the Hummer earlier, the one who had given her a visual orgasm at the stoplight.

She knew for a fact that he wasn't volunteering on the manhunt—a black man in this neck of the woods, after sundown? Hell no! Oh, she thought, this brother is definitely being hunted. Sunni knew that if he was caught only one of two things could happen: one, he would be shot dead on the spot, another black man out of the running; or two, he would go straight to jail and the key would be thrown away.

Guydamn, Sunni contemplated. *Why'd he have to end up on* my *doorstep? What am I supposed to do?*

As she watched him looking for a way out, somewhere to run, his face clammy with sweat, her heart went out to him. She quickly ran to the back door, unlocked it and called out, "Come on, come on, I got you!" She waved her arm, motioning him to hurry up.

She shook her head, knowing that she had let her emotions override her intellect.

Upon seeing the door open, Trill ran inside. He couldn't believe it. He knew that it was only a matter of seconds before they had his black butt hemmed in. This lady being here at the right place, at the right time—he didn't know if it was a setup or what. But for now he was grateful to be able to get some heat and a spot to hide. She slammed the door shut, locking both the security door and the entry door.

He inhaled a deep breath to try catch his breath and said, "Damn, you saved my ass. Anybody see me?"

Sunni looked out the still open blinds in the kitchen. She separated the blinds just enough to peek out. The coast appeared to be clear. Sunni then closed all the blinds in her house and drew the drapes.

"You can hang out here if you need to," Sunni said flatly when she returned to the kitchen. "You need to use the phone or something?"

"Naw, I just need to lay low and chill for a minute," Trill said and then plopped down on her oversized yellow chaise, exhausted, dehydrated and hungry. Then he thought again. "You got a cell?"

Sunni nodded as she reached for her cell and handed it to him. She listened as he gave someone demands to report his truck stolen. After Trill ended the call, he sat there with a bit of slight anxiety, thinking about the stash box, wondering if the tow company would find it and rip it off. Sunni noticed that his mind was somewhere else, so she tried to redirect attention.

"Well, I was just about to eat some hot wings," she said casually. "Have some?"

"You got something cold to drink?" he asked. Writing off any negative thoughts about the drugs being gone, he knew he had the best secret hiding place money could buy.

"Sure." She walked over to a cabinet that sat behind the yellow loveseat. She opened the refridgerater, introducing a complete stock of liquor, most of which hadn't been uncapped. She then hollered back to Trill.

"I have Coke, Sprite, Corona, Hennessy, Moët, Remy, Grey Goose, orange juice, basically whatever you want," Sunni said, naming the drinks as she scanned the fridge then glanced over to her bar.

"Hennie's good, give me a shot of that on ice." He could feel her eyes burning into him, so he added, "Please."

As she grabbed a glass from the cabinet and poured Trill's drink, she decided that maybe she'd have a drink, too. No use in having dude drinking alone, she thought. After pouring herself a Grey Goose and cranberry, she headed to the kitchen and grabbed some ice from the freezer. When she closed the freezer door and went to turn around, Trill was already standing in the kitchen. He pulled off his sweater and tossed it across the chair beside him as if he lived there. Trill's body caught Sunni off guard. Seeing him in that black wife beater, she could see he'd definitely spent a lot of time working on his body. *Penitentiary body* she thought as he drunk the Henni like it was a shot.

BABY BROTHER

By 50 Cent and Noire

Prison number: 837R2006

Height: six feet, one inch

Face front.

(flash)

Turn to your left.

(flash)

Now to your right.

(flash)

"Good morning, New York! It's time to get the hell outta bed! Right about now you're waking up with my girl Jonesy! Sure we hired her because she's pretty ... but then after talking to her I realized she also has a great rap! Wake up on Hot 97! Let's get ta grinding on this hot, sunny morning in the Big Apple!"

The early morning sun baked the run-down five-story tenement from the direction of Queens. On the second floor, thin red curtains swayed in the light breeze, and the B20 to Spring Creek groaned toward Linden Boulevard, traces of its exhaust fumes wafting through the open window.

Inside the bedroom, Baby Brother plunged into his wet yummy, bumping bone and scraping walls. "Yeahhhh," he groaned, getting his mash on. He took a deep breath, then grunted and arched his back, pounding his pipe.

Beneath him, Sari moaned and panted. Her dark hair curled around her face and fanned over the pillow. Her juices smelled like Fruity Pebbles and it was just about breakfast time.

"Right there, mami?" Baby Brother demanded, veins bulging, flinging sweat. "Is that where you like it, baby? Right there?"

She tossed her head no, but still squealed in pleasure as he grabbed her toned thighs, spreading them apart in a wide V. His fingers were hot on her caramel-colored skin. She pulled him deeper into her, then whispered something nasty in Spanish as the headboard slammed against the wall and Miss Jonesy talked shit in the background.

"Cool," Baby Brother said, withdrawing until only the head was left inside. It pulsed and throbbed in the rim of her tight opening as he extended his arms and balanced himself on the palms of his hands. "If the dick ain't good to ya, then I might as well take it out."

She squeezed her legs tight. "No!"

He laughed. "Then let me hear you say this dick is good!"

"Sshh!" She stopped rolling her ass and frowned. "Why you gotta say 'dick' so loud like that! Tony might hear you!"

Baby Brother laughed again. "Fuck Tony."

Sari giggled and slapped his arm. Working her hips into a hard grind, she pulled him deeply into her soft gushy, then wrapped her long legs around his back as her teeth found his nipple. She swirled her wet tongue around his bud and sucked gently, her lips pressed firmly against the hard muscle of his chest.

Baby Brother clenched his jaw and shuddered. "Aaah, baby. Damn. Shit. Slow down. *Goddamn*. Slow down, mami! Damn, you throwing some good-ass stuff around, girl."

It was sticky and hot inside her box, and he didn't wanna move. He forced himself to pull out of her, then slid down her body, sighing. He paused to lick her stiff, light-brown nipple, then continued south, lapping sweat from the crevice of her belly button before pressing his face deeply into her wet spot.

"Yummy . . ." He smacked his lips between licks. Her juice was like honey. Sweet and thick, and he wished he could put his whole head up inside her.

Sari gasped. Her muscles went rigid as he made waves of pleasure flow from her center. She held tight to his head and opened her mouth. A Spanish pleasure tirade exploded from her lips and filled the whole room. "Aaah, baby! Yeah, just like that. Right there, just like that." Then, moments later, "Oooweee, too deep! No, harder. Yeah. *Just like that!*" And then finally, "Oooh. Damn. Yeah. Damn! Why you gotta leave me, huh, Zabu? Why you gotta go? I love you, Z. You know that, don't you?"

Baby Brother moaned, spurting the last of himself into her warmth. He rolled onto his side and pulled her into his dark arms. He gazed into her flashing eyes, and despite the way their bodies had just battled, he saw the deep pain that was lurking there.

He kissed her damp curls and squeezed her closer. "I *gotta* go, girl. That's what's real. This ghetto's gonna kill me if I don't. But I'm coming back for you, Sari. That's truth, baby. That's truth."

■

Baby Brother stood up. He used a bunch of Wet Wipes to clean himself, then kissed Sari again and got dressed. It was time to go. Priest was waiting for him back at the crib, and they had moves to make.

"I'ma get up with you later, cool? I'll be waiting downstairs around six. Have your fine ass ready too, 'cause the West Indian Day Parade draws niggas from all over Brooklyn and there won't be noplace to park near Eastern Parkway."

He winked at Sari, then walked over to the half-open window and raised it all the way up. He glanced down at the sparkling whip parked below, in the exact same condition in which he had left it in the night before. While her eyes were on him he pretended he was climbing out the window and onto the raggedy fire escape, but then turned around real fast and walked over to the door instead. He heard her shocked intake of breath as he reached for the knob.

"Z! What the hell you doing?" She jumped up, her eyes flashing with alarm. He liked it when she got all hyped. Her nature was a perfect indicator of her ethnic mix. Black and Hispanic. She was a down chick and had a temper on her, too. "Don't open that damn door! You gotta go out the window!" She snatched the sheet off the bed and tried to wrap it around her nakedness. "Man, Tony's home! You can't let him see you leaving outta my room!"

Baby Brother grinned and walked out, closing the door on her high-pitched protests. Fuck all that window action. He was leaving out the door today.

His light-brown eyes danced and his skin looked chocolatey smooth against the red-and-white Rocawear shirt he wore. He hiked up his jeans until they settled over his Air Force Ones just the right way, then headed down the short hall toward the front door.

Passing the kitchen, he stuck his head inside, then slammed his hand against the side of the refrigerator as hard as he could. A cracking sound exploded in the air, startling the handsome Puerto Rican killer sitting at the table. Out of nowhere, a small silver gat appeared in the man's hand.

"Damn, Tony! What? You gon' shoot me, or something?"

Tony stared at him with a snarl and set the gun down on the chair between his thighs. Even in the heat his voice came out feeling like ice.

"Yo, muthafucka. What the fuck is you doin' in my crib?"

Baby Brother checked out Sari's half-brother. Her father had been black, and while she was brown and curly-haired, Tony was a pale Hispanic with dark, piercing eyes. He'd been sitting alone in the kitchen smoking a dutchey and counting a large stack of chips. His jet-black hair was shower-wet, his bare chest stained with tattoos and bulging with jailhouse muscle. A large baggie half-filled with white powder sat on the table in front of him, and another, much smaller bag rested on a triple-beam scale.

"Damn. Whatever happened to 'Good morning,' man?"

Tony pushed the stack of money aside and reached into his back pocket. The glint of his knife caught Baby Brother's eye.

"Yo. You been up in my joint all night?" His voice was deadly. "Back there witcha dick up in my little sister?" He twirled his knife. The tip of his blunt glared red, and his cold eyes never left Baby Brother's face. "You must be a bad motherfucker then, huh?"

Baby Brother laughed and held up his hands. "Chill, *amigo*. I ain't the enemy, man. Shit, after three years I'm just about family. Plus, I'm about to be outtie in a minute. No disrespect to your crib or nothing. I just wanted to spend some time with Sari. You know, treat her right before I leave, man."

Tony stopped twirling the knife. Baby Brother knew how sharp that blade was. Tony was almost as legendary as the Monster had been on the knife tip. Both of them had plenty of carved-up victims walking the streets.

"That's right, I forgot. You graduated. Now you runnin' off to college to be some kinda fuckin' professor or something." He laughed coldly. "That's real stupid, yo. You need to claim you some territory and be a real man now, homey. You can fuck my little sister in my crib, then come stand in my kitchen where I can smell your nuts? Yeah, you a fuckin' man. But real men pay dues, amigo! Leave that college business for the herbs out in Canarsie and get yourself a grind. Business is good on this side of the bridge. Tell ya pretty-ass brothers you coming to work for me now."

"Man, what I look like? You can kill all that shit. I got plans. I ain't slinging rock for nobody. Not for you, not for that stupid nigga Borne, and not for my brothers neither."

Tony laughed. "Okay, okay, I tell you what! I'm a nice guy. Those fuckin' twins can come work for me too, cool? You can be my runner, and your brothers can be my capos. You can hold my balls while they take turns suckin' my dick!" He laughed louder this time, sweeping half the bills off the table and to the floor as he gripped his knife in his fist and glared.

Baby Brother watched him for a moment, then walked toward the door shaking his head. Tony had been tryna get at him for years, but it was cool. He was the oldest boy in the Santiago family, and Sari was the youngest and only girl. It was only right that he would look out for his little sister the same way the six older Davis brothers came to the table for him.

Baby Brother and Sari had been rolling together since he was in the tenth grade and she was in the ninth. They were on opposite sides of a family rivalry. The Davis twins, Farad and Finesse, controlled the rock and the powder flowing in and out of Brownsville and were well-known for their savage brutality. The Santos clan ran the streets of East New York, with Tony at the helm. He was ruthless and crazy. A cutter. Like the Monster. A loose missile just itching to launch. There was no love lost between the two families, but they tolerated each other. Mainly on account of business, and partly because of Baby Brother and Sari.

Baby Brother walked down the hall and went through the stairwell door. The hot smell of stale urine and beer rushed out at him. He maneuvered around a couple of winos and crackheads who were sitting on the stairs trying to come down off their all-night highs.

"Whassup, Felix. Big Porter. How you doin' this morning, Mrs. Woodson?"

The woman he addressed beamed at him. She was Jelly's moms, a dude he knew from way back in the day. They'd boxed together at the BBC gym, but Jelly had gone into the Marine Corps two years ago, and it wasn't long after that that the streets had claimed his mother.

"Baby Brother!" the woman exclaimed. She pulled her bra strap up on her shoulder and tried to smooth her hair.

"You almost ready to leave us, huh?" She nudged the crackhead sitting next to her. "This boy right here is something else. He used to be Jelly's best friend, you know. He was the only kid who ever whupped my Jelly in the ring too. Now he's going off to college to learn how to be an astronaut! Ain't that right, Baby Brother?"

He smiled down at her. Her hair was raggedy and her teeth looked like rotten little worms, but Baby Brother showed her much respect.

"Nah, Mrs. Woodson. I'm gonna be a surgeon. I'm majoring in pre-med." The odors assaulting him were excruciatingly foul, but he withstood them. He stood there and carried on a conversation with Mrs. Woodson the same way he used to when his boy Jelly had still been around. He talked to her the way he used to talk to her back when she was still a loud-mouthed, heavyset, dark-skinned woman holding her family down in a cool apartment off of New Lots Avenue and pushing a decent whip. As cracked-out as Mrs. Woodson was now, and as dreadful as she smelled, Baby Brother treated her the same way he would've wanted somebody to treat his own mother—if he'd had one.

"Boy, you got a future ahead of you," Jelly's moms told him. "A real future. Wherever you goin' to school, hurr'up and get there. This place ain't for boys like you. Don't let it crush you like it done crushed me."

■

Baby Brother stepped out of the building and into the hazy sunshine. He inhaled the morning air and gazed at the candy-red 2007 drop-top Mercedes parked at the curb. The whip was just like he'd left it, and he wasn't surprised. Everybody in Central Brooklyn knew Farad's wheels when they saw them, and only a fool with a death wish would have laid a finger on the paint.

"Baby Brother!"

His name rang out from a doorway across the street.

"You tell that nigga Farad his g-ride ain't as tight as mine!"

Baby Brother grinned and lifted his chin at the skinny brother standing on the stoop. It was Bip, one of Farad's ex-partners. A guy who had grown up with the Davis brothers in Brownsville but who slummed around in East New York now. Bip had been banned from Brownsville on Farad's direct word, and had been allowed to keep his life only because they'd been dawgs damn near from the cradle. But even that wouldn't stop Farad from having him murked if he got caught crossing over into The Ville.

"That's truth, Bip. I'ma let him know that shit too."

"Yeah. Let him know I been up watching his whip all

night, yo. Tell him he owe me! If it wasn't for me, some base-head prolly woulda ran off with his spinners."

Baby Brother unlocked the car and climbed behind the wheel. It was a quality ride, paid for with cash dollars. Farad had it detailed every three days, and it smelled factory-fresh at all times. He settled into the seat, then slid the key into the ignition and listened to the engine purr.

He drove down the streets of East New York with the top down, driving aimlessly and absorbing the hood vibe. N.J.S. beats blared from the speakers as Reem Raw killed a hot track with illa New York lyrics. He rode up Shepherd, crossed Linden Boulevard, and headed toward New Lots. It was early, but niggas was already out on the hot streets scheming on their next hustle.

Baby Brother nodded at a few familiar faces as he cruised down the block. He stopped at a light on the corner of Hegeman Avenue. A couple of gangsta-looking niggas with larceny in their eyes grilled him as they walked by. Baby Brother was up on them. He knew what they were thinking and hoped they were smart enough to think again. He was a hard nigga, good with his hands. He'd come up on the streets in the gym, trained by his brothers to get in close and handle his.

But with two days left in New York he wasn't trying to get into nothing hot except some more of Sari's yummy. He pumped the volume even higher and decided to let Farad's whip speak loud and clear to anybody who might wanna get smoked.

On the way home he thought a lot about college and about Sari, too. Leaving her was gonna be hard, but he knew it would pay off in the end. A degree from Stanford came with certain guarantees, and although he was gonna miss the comfort of having his brothers around, he was grateful for the opportunity to escape the urban jungle. It was what their mother would have wanted. Their father, too.

Pulling over at a corner candy store beneath the Number 3 El, Baby Brother went inside and bought a soda and a bag of pretzels. When he came back out a bunch of kids were admiring Farad's whip. He let them climb inside and blow the horn and push a few buttons and shit, then he got behind the wheel again and made his way back to The Ville, where his brothers waited.

Priest had just finished his breakfast of buttery grits and eggs when the front door slammed. Three of Farad's soldiers were posted outside, and relief flooded Priest as he heard familiar footsteps approaching. Baby Brother had stayed in East New York all night long, and even though the kid was eighteen now, Priest still worried about him, especially out there messing around with them treacherous Puerto Ricans.

"Zabu!" he called out, his voice heavy and full of bass. "You late, man. I told you I was gon' take you to get some suitcases today, but if you wanna haul your gear to Cali in some black garbage bags, you can do that, you know."

Despite his bark, Priest's eyes were full of pride as his youngest brother strolled into the kitchen. Just like his six brothers, Baby Brother was tall, with deep mahogany skin and amber eyes. He was muscled up and perfectly cut, and although they all worked out hard, the majestic physique was just part of their genetics.

Priest was the oldest, and the most battle-scarred. He had raised the other boys after their mother died, and Baby Brother was his heart. His favorite. His salvation. Priest couldn't help it. These days he served as an assistant pastor of a small storefront church, operated his own barbershop up on Rockaway Avenue, and gave Bible lessons at a youth center twice a week.

But he had a past that just couldn't be wiped clean. He had pimped women, slung rock, slumped foes, organized gangs, and hustled the hell outta the game. But looking at Baby Brother killed all those past demons. His little brother was his pride and joy. Hard evidence that despite all the grimy capers Priest had pulled, all the prey he'd bitten, and all the upstate prison time he'd served, somehow God had favored him and allowed him to redeem himself and do something right. Every time he looked at Baby Brother, Priest saw the man that he himself should have been.

"What it do, 'Twan." Baby Brother gave him some dap on his way to the refrigerator.

"You late, man. I told you we was leaving at nine."

Baby Brother flashed him a grin and rubbed his stomach. "I'm hungry, tho'. Gotta stick something in my belly before we roll."

Priest opened the microwave and took out one of four paper plates he'd covered in Saran Wrap. "Here." He set it on the table. "Put ya face in this and hurry up. I gotta be back for services this afternoon."

"Aiight. Yo, why's it so quiet in here? Where is everybody?"

Priest shrugged. "You know the scene, man. When you do your work under the dark of night, you gotta regroup when it's light. The twins are both upstairs. Matter fact, Malik's gon' be here in a minute. Go upstairs and tell them two knuckleheads to get down here and eat."

Ten minutes later Priest sat at the head of the table watching four of his young brothers grub. Malik had arrived dressed in his NYPD blues. As they dug into the plates he'd prepared for them, Priest couldn't help but smile inside. It felt good to sit at the same table with his cats. Raheem had taken a trip for the long weekend, and Kadir was down in the A.C. doing his thing, but with Baby Brother leaving for college in a couple of days, both of them would be showing up to see him off.

"Snatch 'em!" Malik hollered real loud.

"Guard ya plate!" Baby Brother threw his arms on the table, encircling his breakfast with wary eyes.

"Man, keep your hands off my damn food!" Farad complained, setting his fork down. "I ain't playin that 'snatch 'em' shit today, dawg. You betta chill with that."

Malik laughed and stuck the stolen slice of turkey bacon in his mouth. "You ain't gotta play nothing but defense, man. You know the rules, muhfuckah! Lose ya heat, I snatch ya meat!" Laughter rang out around the table, and Farad reacted quickly.

"Snatch 'em!"

Finesse cursed as his twin snatched a crisp slice of bacon off his plate and started crunching.

"You getting slow, nigga." Farad chuckled. "I coulda got me two pieces off you, yo."

Priest laughed along with them, but his heart was heavy. He had prayed for a better life for his brothers. Nothing would make him happier than seeing Farad and Finesse out of the game and doing something legitimate with their skills. He'd dreamed of opening a chain of barbershops and installing one of his brothers at the helm of each operation, but Raheem and Malik both had good jobs with benefits, Kadir was hooked on card tables, and neither of the twins was interested in a nine-to-five. Priest stood up and refilled Baby Brother's glass from a container of juice on the counter.

"So," he said, looking around the table before nodding at his youngest brother. "Everybody 'bout ready to get rid of this lil' cat? Ain't but two days left, then he's out."

Finesse shrugged. "I'd rather see him bounce for a minute than have him scrambling yay like them niggas on the stoop. Shit, B-Brother. You gone be on some real West Coast shit when you get back. You sure you can't go to school somewhere in New York? Maybe upstate?"

"I can go almost anywhere I wanna go," Baby Brother said. "But Stanford is giving up the best scholarship package, man. Plus it's a top school. I'd be crazy to let something like this slide by me."

Malik nodded, wiping his mouth. "That's what's real, man. Graduate from Stanford with a degree in shit shoveling, and you still considered a heavyweight in the corporate world. Fuck around with one of these city schools, and you might end up working for Transit or coming on the force, or worse—following Ra down to Corrections and getting on over there." He tossed his plate in the trash. "Cali is a good bet for you. Go for it. We got your back."

"Yeah," Farad said, standing up with his empty plate in his hand. He reached over and punched Baby Brother on his shoulder, then mushed his head like he was ten years old again. "Just make sure you put some damn gas in my car before you fly, though. Shit! I'm glad that nigga leaving. I'ma finally get a chance to push my own whip."

Malik headed for the door. "Yo, Ant, what time we flying outta here on Monday?"

"Seven. I already told Ra to be here by four. That'll put us at JFK way before five."

"Cool." Malik nodded. "I'll get wit'chall in a few. They got me pulling a double shift, so it's gonna be a long night."

Fifteen minutes later two of the Davis brothers were ready to hit downtown Brooklyn. Priest let Baby Brother drive. He couldn't bring himself to get behind the wheel of Farad's drug-bought car. Negativity was all up in it, and he wanted no part of that.

Also by

K. ELLIOTT

Middle school teacher Dream Nelson has a seemingly perfect life, but she has one weakness—thugs. Follow Dream and her drug trafficking boyfriend Jamal as they live the bling lifestyle with expensive cars, jewels, and trips. Naïve Dream soon learns there is a price to pay for the lavishness.

One million dollars and Tommy Fatboy Dupree can invest this money in real estate and be finished with the drug game. Seems easy enough, right? Tommy has two obstacles, one that is obvious to him—the DEA that he knows is on his trail—the other not so apparent. Tommy soon learns that JoJo and Twin, his childhood buddies, aren't really his friends. One man is sleeping with his girlfriend and the other sets him up to be robbed.

Ordering information www.k-elliott.com or www.beststreetfiction.com

15831